R.L. STINE'S

GHOSTS OF
FEAR STREET

REVENGE OF THE
SHADOW PEOPLE

—AND—

THE BUGMAN
LIVES!

R. L. STINE'S

GHOSTS OF
FEAR STREET ®

REVENGE OF THE
SHADOW PEOPLE

—AND—

THE BUGMAN
LIVES!

TWICE TERRIFYING TALES

ALADDIN
NEW YORK LONDON TORONTO SYDNEY

This book is a work of fiction. Any references to historical events, real people, or real locales are used fictitiously. Other names, characters, places, and incidents are the product of the author's imagination, and any resemblance to actual events or locales or persons, living or dead, is entirely coincidental.

ALADDIN

An imprint of Simon & Schuster Children's Publishing Division
1230 Avenue of the Americas, New York, NY 10020
This Aladdin paperback edition August 2010
Revenge of the Shadow People copyright © 1996 by Parachute Press, Inc.
Revenge of the Shadow People written by Jahnna N. Malcolm
The Bugman Lives! copyright © 1996 by Parachute Press, Inc.
The Bugman Lives! written by Carol Gorman
All rights reserved, including the right
of reproduction in whole or in part in any form.
ALADDIN is a trademark of Simon & Schuster, Inc., and related
logo is a registered trademark of Simon & Schuster, Inc.
FEAR STREET is a registered trademark of Parachute Press, Inc.
For information about special discounts for bulk purchases, please
contact Simon & Schuster Special Sales at 1-866-506-1949
or business@simonandschuster.com.
The Simon & Schuster Speakers Bureau can bring authors to your live event.
For more information or to book an event contact the Simon & Schuster Speakers
Bureau at 1-866-248-3049 or visit our website at www.simonspeakers.com.
Manufactured in the United States of America 1110 OFF
2 4 6 8 10 9 7 5 3
Library of Congress Control Number 2009940370
ISBN 978-1-4424-0802-9
These titles were previously published individually by Pocket Books.

REVENGE OF THE SHADOW PEOPLE

"I'm telling you, Vinny, it was *totally* gross. It chased me all around Fear Lake, dripping thick, green snot. I never saw anything like it."

My friend Bobby Beasley's lips trembled as he told me another one of his stories. This one was about the swamp monster of Fear Lake.

"It stood twelve feet tall—a huge tower of green snot," Bobby continued. "And it had all these long, stringy tentacles for arms."

Bobby stretched out his arms and waved them in the air, nearly poking me in the eye.

"I ran as fast as I could, but the monster grabbed me—with one of its slimy tentacles. Like this—"

Bobby grabbed my arm and I jumped.

"I kicked the monster hard—as hard as I could. It let out a horrible shriek. Then it slithered back into the lake, shrieking the whole way."

"Wow!" I said. I started to breathe again. I hadn't realized I had been holding my breath.

Bobby went on. "That was two years ago," he said in a hushed voice. "The monster hasn't been seen since. But he's down there—waiting."

Bobby gave a serious nod and tugged on his baseball cap.

My mouth dropped open.

Sometimes Bobby's stories really scare me—like now. He tells lots and lots of creepy stories—because he's seen lots and lots of monsters. I live only a few blocks from Bobby, but I've never seen any monsters. And boy, am I glad. I don't know what I'd do if I even met *one*.

Bobby always saves his best stories for after school. That's why I like walking home with him.

"A big, green snot monster? Oh, please," Sharon Lipp mumbled, tossing her long blond braid over her shoulder. Sharon always walks home with us, but she thinks Bobby's stories are dumb. "He doesn't expect us to believe this stupid stuff, does he?" she whispered.

"I believe him," I told her.

Sharon rolled her big brown eyes and nudged me

hard with her elbow. She caught me in the ribs. Which hurt. Sharon is really skinny, but she's really strong.

"Bobby, you should carry a camera with you all the time—the way I do." Sharon pointed to the camera dangling around her neck. "Then we could actually *see* these monsters."

"Uh. Yeah. That's a good idea," Bobby said.

"So, what did you do after the big snot monster disappeared?" Sharon went on.

Bobby squinted at Sharon from beneath the visor of his cap. "I called the cops and filed a full report with Detective Flynn. Me and the detective are like this." Bobby held up two fingers pressed together. "I talk to him at least once a week."

"I bet Detective Flynn *loves* to hear from you," Sharon said, smirking.

Bobby didn't seem to notice. "Sure does. The police really need my help on these weird cases."

"You've seen more ghosts and weird stuff than anybody I know," I said. "Doesn't it . . . scare you?"

Bobby shrugged. "That's what I get for living on Fear Street."

Just the mention of Fear Street made my palms a little sweaty. I dug my hands into my pockets.

"Vinny," Bobby leaned close and whispered.

"Did I ever tell you about the time I accidentally wandered into the Fear Street Woods after dark?"

I shook my head no.

"Do you want to know what happened?" Bobby asked, his voice still low.

I nodded yes.

Bobby bared his teeth and raised his hands as if they were claws. "Werewolf!" he leaped at us and snarled.

Sharon and I both jumped this time. Sharon swung her lunch box at him. "Cut that out, Bobby. That's not funny."

"I didn't say it was. No one ever laughs about the Fear Street werewolf," he said in a spooky voice. "Catch you later!"

We had reached Park Drive—the street where Bobby turned right to go home—to his house on Fear Street.

"See you!" I shouted back.

"Bobby says he knows all this scary stuff about Shadyside. But he makes it all up," Sharon said as we walked on.

"Well, maybe he makes up some of it. But so what?" I asked. "Bobby's a good guy. And I like his creepy stories." I glanced over my shoulder toward Fear Street and shivered.

4

"He makes up *all* of it," Sharon declared. "A careful listener can tell when someone is lying. Besides, creepy things like that just don't happen."

I didn't know how wrong Sharon was about that. But we were both about to find out.

2

Sharon and I jogged across my lawn and dropped our backpacks on the floor in the hall. Sharon's parents both work, so she always comes to my house for an after-school snack.

Sharon set her lunch box on top of her pack. But she kept her camera on. It dangled around her neck on its black strap—as it always does.

Sharon got the camera two months ago, on her twelfth birthday. A gift from her grandparents. She's worn it every day since. "A good photographer is never without her camera," she says.

"Hi, Mom! Hi, Dad!" I called out. My parents are both architects. Their office is in the basement of our house.

But they hardly spend time down there anymore.

As usual, their attention was totally taken up by one thing. They didn't even turn around when Sharon and I walked in.

"Goo-goo goo-goo," they babbled at the new star of our family. Eighteen-month-old Baby Joey.

Sharon says Joey looks like a mini version of me. Which makes me nuts. We both have black hair and blue eyes. But Joey is really chunky. I like to think of myself as muscular.

"Hello, Mr. and Mrs. Salvo!" Sharon tried to get their attention.

No reply. Not even a wave.

"Don't bother," I muttered. I grabbed two apples from the bowl on the living room table and tossed one to Sharon. "It would take an atomic bomb to tear them away from Joey."

I stuck my tongue out at my parents. I couldn't help it.

Joey stared at me over Dad's shoulder with his big blue eyes. He saw my face and giggled.

"Hey, did you hear that?" Dad cried. "Joey laughed."

"Gah-gin," Joey said. In baby talk that means "Again."

"Gah-gin," he repeated, pointing at me.

Dad and Mom finally turned to look at us.

"Oh, Vinny, you're home," Mom said. "And Sharon, too."

I rolled my eyes. "Yeah, we just got in."

Dad didn't say hi. Or even ask how school was. All he said was "Vinny, wait till you see Joey's new trick." He stood my brother on the floor beside the playpen. "Okay, Joey, let's see you be a bear."

Joey bent over, put both hands on the floor, and made a gurgling sound. My parents doubled over with laughter. They hugged Joey. Then they hugged each other.

I wanted to barf.

"Listen, Dad, I need to ask you about my soccer game Saturday. The coach wants me to play striker, and I'm—"

"Sadow!" Joey suddenly squealed. "Sadow!"

"Quiet, Joey," I said.

The smile vanished from my dad's face. "Vincent, that's no way to talk to your brother. He's trying to communicate with you."

I let out a long sigh. "Sadow to you, too, Joe."

"You know he means shadow, Vinny. Now, be a good sport and make that shadow Joey loves so much," Dad ordered.

When I was a kid, I loved making shadow puppets. In fact, I couldn't stop. I made them all the time—in school, at home, in the dentist's office, everywhere.

My favorite shadow—and my best one—was the

8

donkey shadow. Now that I'm twelve, I don't like making the shadows anymore. In fact, I think it's really geeky.

But Joey loves my donkey shadow. So now, whether I want to or not, I have to make them. Whenever Joey wants.

"Sharon and I have to do our homework," I muttered between clenched teeth.

"Make the shadow," Dad said firmly. "Joey likes it."

"Pwease!" Joey cried. He gazed up at me with his big eyes. A string of drool dribbled down from the bottom of his lip to his blue terry-cloth sleeper.

"Okay. Okay." I sighed. I marched over to the brass lamp standing behind Dad's recliner and aimed the light at the wall. Then I laced my fingers together and shoved them into the beam of light.

There it was—on the wall. As always, I made the perfect donkey shadow.

"Donkey!" Joey squealed, clapping his hands together. He clapped so hard he fell over backward. Everybody laughed. I did, too. I couldn't help it.

"Gah-gin!" Joey cooed.

I shoved my hands back together and wiggled my fingers for ears. The same thing happened. Joey clapped, fell over, and we all laughed.

"Oh, dear, the chicken is cooking and I forgot

9

about the vegetables!" Mom suddenly cried. She tapped Dad on the arm. "James, come help me."

"You stay here with your big brother and Sharon while Mommy and I make dinner," Dad said to Joey. "Vinny will make more sadows for you."

"But, Dad—" I started to protest.

Dad disappeared into the kitchen.

"Let's take him upstairs so I can see your new computer," Sharon suggested.

Sharon and I carried Joey upstairs to my room. The second I placed him on the bed, he cried, "Sadows! Sadows!"

"Don't you ever give up?" I asked with an annoyed sigh.

Joey clapped his hands together and giggled.

"I'll pull down the shade and you make a shadow for him," Sharon said. "The best shadow is made with only one light source."

Sharon is always saying stuff like that—as if she knows everything. Some of the kids in school think it's annoying. But I think it's sort of funny.

Sharon pulled down the shade, and I flicked on the red reading lamp next to my bed. I twisted it so the light shone on the wall above my headboard. Then I made a big show of doing another donkey.

"Hee-haw!" I added, wiggling the donkey's ears.

Joey squealed with delight.

"Okay. That's the last one." I dropped my hands and shoved them in my pockets.

Joey's eyes were still glued to the wall behind my bed.

So were Sharon's.

"Whoa," Sharon whispered, her brown eyes two huge circles. "Cool!"

I faced the wall—and gasped.

My hands were in my pockets—but my donkey shadow was still on the wall!

3

"**W**ow!" I stared down at my hands and then back at the wall. The donkey shadow still floated there. "How did I do *that?*"

"Something else in the room is doing it," Sharon said.

"That has to be it," I agreed. I slowly spun in a circle, searching for a piece of furniture, a coat hanging on a chair—anything that could cast a donkey shadow. "I don't see anything. Do you?"

"No," Sharon replied, gazing around. "I don't."

We stared at each other, then back at the wall.

The shadow floated there.

It was the weirdest, coolest thing I had ever seen.

And then the donkey's ears flickered. At least I thought they did. I stared hard at the wall, but the shadow remained still.

"Hey, let's show it to your parents. They're architects. They know all about angles and stuff. It probably has something to do with the angle of the light shining on the wall." Sharon headed for the door.

"Come on, Joey." I scooped my brother off the bed. "Let's find Mom and Dad. I bet Sharon's right. Mom and Dad can figure this out."

Sharon and I pounded down the steps. Mom and Dad heard us and met us at the bottom of the staircase.

"What's the matter?" Mom cried, taking my brother from my arms. "Is Joey all right?"

"Joey's fine," I told her. "It's my wall."

"Your wall?" Dad asked.

"Well, not really my wall. I made a donkey shadow—and it's still there—on the wall." I grabbed Dad's arm and pulled him up the steps. "You have to see it!"

"It really is unbelievable," Sharon said, following us up the stairs. "Of course, there's a scientific theory that explains the whole thing. Right, Mr. Salvo?"

"Hmmm," Dad mumbled. "Let's have a look."

13

Mom came, too, carrying Joey. We all crowded into the room.

"See? It's right . . ."

The words caught in my throat.

The shadow was gone.

"Dad, it was there. Really! Ask Sharon."

"It was there, Mr. Salvo." Sharon backed me up. "I saw it—and so did Joey."

"I believe you," Dad said. "Both of you. I've seen these kinds of shadows before."

"Really? Where?" I asked.

"In a museum. In an exhibit that had a special light," he explained. "It made your shadow stick to the wall. Even after you moved away. Something like that must have happened here."

Dad moved around my room, investigating. We watched him. He tilted my bedside lamp and flicked it off and on. "No. This light couldn't have done it. This is just a regular lightbulb."

"Da Da! Go!" Baby Joey squealed. He held his arms out to my dad.

"What is it, Joey?" Dad cooed. "Did the big, bad shadow scare you? No, you're a big boy. Too big to be scared of a silly shadow." Dad took Joey from my mom and headed out of the room.

Sharon held her camera up to one eye and pointed it at the wall. "I wish I'd taken a picture of that shadow. A good photographer has to think of these things."

Mom smiled. "Dinner will be ready soon, Vin." She followed Dad out of the room.

A little later Sharon left, and Mom called upstairs to tell me dinner was ready.

I started to head downstairs—but I turned back.

I had to try to make another shadow. I had to see if the same thing happened again.

The bedside lamp was still on.

I slipped my hands into the light.

I clasped my fingers together and made my donkey shadow.

Staring hard at the wall, I held my hands there for a full minute.

Then I held my breath and slowly removed them from the light.

4

Nothing.

The wall was blank.

No donkey shadow.

Too bad, I thought. Those shadows would be totally cool if they stayed there.

I headed downstairs for dinner.

The time between dessert and going to bed was my favorite—because Baby Joey was in his crib by seven o'clock every night. I didn't have to listen to any more goo-goo talk until morning.

I did my homework and watched some TV. Then I went up to bed. I stretched out under my blanket and stared at the ceiling. It glimmered with glow-in-the-dark stars. Dad and I stuck them up there two years ago to help me learn the constellations. Of course, that was B.J.—Before Joey.

I was staring up at Orion, the constellation right above my head, when I noticed a dark shapeless shadow falling over some of the stars.

I don't remember ever seeing that shape on my ceiling before, I thought.

Sometimes at night the light from the street lamp outside my window casts shadows in my room. But they usually fall on my wall. Once in a while a shadow will travel across the ceiling. But only if a car drives past.

I sat up on my elbows and gazed around the room. A heap of rumpled clothes was on the chair in front of the window. I stared up at the shadow—then back at the pile of clothes.

That's it, I realized. The clothes are casting the shadow.

I padded over to the chair and pounded the pile with my fist. It was totally flat now.

I checked the ceiling.

The shadow hadn't changed.

Hmmmm. What else could be making the shadow?

I scanned the room and spotted Sluggo the Gorilla and Leonard the Lion—two of Joey's stuffed animals—sitting on my dresser.

I knocked them to the floor.

I checked the ceiling.

The shadow was still there.

My stomach started to knot up.

It's just a shadow, I told myself. Nothing to be afraid of. But when I jumped back into bed, I made sure I didn't look up.

I fluffed up my pillows and reached for my comforter. I started to lie down—but something caught my eye.

Something quivering on the ceiling.

I quickly glanced up—and gasped.

The shadow was growing.

I yanked the covers up to my chin and watched as the dark shape slowly spread across the stars.

There's a logical explanation for this, I tried to convince myself. There has to be.

I stared at the shadow. Stared as it continued to grow and shift. Taking some sort of shape.

A head seemed to be forming. A bear's head, I thought at first.

No.

The shadow stretched up. Up in two places—forming horns. Yes, they were definitely horns. A head with horns!

My heart began to pound in my chest.

Shadows can't do this! They can't take any shape they want!

I swallowed hard.

The shadow shifted across the ceiling. The horns lost their shape. Re-formed into another shape. A blurry shape that didn't look like much of anything.

And then I saw an eye appear. And a jaw.

A huge jaw filled with pointed teeth.

I could make out each sharp tooth perfectly.

Then the horns re-formed. Twisted horns that rose up from the shadow head.

I watched in horror as the horns snaked along the ceiling. As the jaw snapped open and closed. As a body began to take shape.

There is no logical explanation for this. I'm getting Mom and Dad now!

I bolted up in bed and threw the blanket off.

I placed one foot on the floor—and a long, black shape swooped down from the ceiling.

It was a claw.

A shadow claw.

It swept across my bed and grabbed for my throat.

5

I opened my mouth to scream.

But the sound didn't have a chance to come out. A flash of light filled the room. Blinding me.

"Vinny, are you still awake?" I heard Mom's voice from the doorway as she switched on the light.

My hand flew to my throat.

Nothing there.

My eyes darted up to the ceiling.

Colored spots from the burst of light floated before me. I squinted hard. The dots started to fade. The stars on the ceiling came into focus. The stars and—nothing else.

The shadow claw was gone.

"Are you okay?" Mom stepped into the room. I could see her clearly now, too. She wore her warm pink robe and fluffy slippers, and her face was filled with concern.

"You're so pale," she said, her brow wrinkled with worry. "Do you feel sick?"

"I'm—I'm okay," I stammered.

She touched the top of my head. "You're all sweaty. Do you think you have a fever?"

I shook my head. "No, no. I'm okay. Really. I'm not sick."

"I don't think you feel warm," Mom agreed.

I glanced nervously around the room, searching for the shadow claw. I didn't see it anywhere.

My room seemed the same as always. The chair under the window held the same rumpled heap of clothes. Sluggo the Gorilla and Leonard the Lion sat on the floor, just where I tossed them. My poster of Cal Ripken breaking Lou Gehrig's consecutive-game record still hung on the wall over my desk.

Everything looked totally normal.

I took a deep breath.

"Did you have a nightmare?" Mom asked. She held me at arm's length and stared at my face.

"Uh-huh." I nodded. What else could I say? A big claw, black and flat like a shadow but razor-sharp, reached out and grabbed my throat—and then it disappeared? Who would believe that?

"Well, try not to think about it," she said, tugging the blanket back over me.

Mom sat down on the corner of my mattress.

"I wanted to know if you would mind babysitting on Friday night?"

I forced a half-smile. "Uh, sure. No problem."

"Good." Mom tucked the covers around me and patted me on the head. "Dad and I want to go on a date. Dinner and a movie, the way we used to *B.K.* — Before Kids."

"Sounds great." I concentrated on keeping my smile.

Mom smiled back, then stood up and headed for the door. "Sleep well," she said and flicked off the light.

I watched her leave the room.

I heard her gently shut my door.

The room instantly darkened.

I gulped and glanced up at the ceiling.

The same ceiling I saw every night. No shadow.

Then why did I feel as if someone — or something — was watching me?

I quickly felt under my bed for my silver Eveready flashlight. I keep it there for late-night reading under the covers.

I flicked on the flashlight. The beam of light caught the ceiling. My dresser. My closet.

Nothing unusual. Still, I had that creepy feeling—as if a pair of staring eyes stalked me.

I clicked off the flashlight. Then I clicked it on again. Having it on made me feel better.

I clutched it to my chest and sat up in bed. I slid up against my headboard, my knees pressed to my chest. I pointed the beam of light out in front of me.

The clock on my dresser said midnight. I felt sleepy. But I couldn't close my eyes. I couldn't stop thinking about that big, black claw reaching for my throat. And now that I was all alone again, it seemed more real than ever. I shivered and pulled the comforter up to my chin.

I stared up at the ceiling.

The head, the horns, the snapping jaw, the body taking shape on my ceiling. I had seen it. I had no doubts.

I knew that monster on my ceiling was real.

And I knew it was still there. Somewhere.

And I knew something else.

I knew it was after me.

6

*B*rrring!

The noise shot straight through my brain. I bolted up in bed, lost my balance, and hit my head against the wall.

I rubbed the sore spot with one hand and shut off the ringing alarm clock with the other. Then I flopped back down on my pillow.

"Yeow!"

I banged my head against the flashlight. Now both sides of my head ached.

What a day. And I wasn't even out of bed yet.

I picked up the flashlight, trying to remember why I had slept with it.

The shadow!

My eyes shot up to the ceiling. Rays of sunlight

streaming in from the window lit up the constellations and made them sparkle.

No shadow.

I sighed with relief—until I glanced at my clock. And groaned. I had not gotten much sleep last night.

I dragged myself out of bed and stumbled into the bathroom. I felt so tired I could hardly push my legs into my jeans. It took all my strength to pull my T-shirt and sweater over my head. Down in the kitchen I swallowed a few spoonfuls of cereal, then headed for school.

When the bell rang, I sat at my desk, my head propped up in my hand. Mr. Ridgely waddled in and stood at the front of the room.

"Good morning, people," he greeted us in his droning voice. "Let's go over last night's reading assignment."

I opened my book and stared down at the page. I tried to focus on the words, but they swam in front of my eyes.

My eyelids began to droop. My head began to nod.

Bang!

I shot up in my seat. My heart thudded in my chest.

Two rows over I spied Bobby bending down to pick up his textbook. "Sorry," he muttered.

I thought Bobby's scare would keep me awake for a while. But it didn't. My eyelids felt like two twenty-pound weights. I couldn't keep them open.

I tried pinching myself whenever they began to close. It worked, but only for a few seconds.

Finally I sat up straight. I stared wide-eyed at my textbook. *Concentrate! Concentrate!* I ordered myself.

But the next thing I knew, I felt a trickle of drool drip down the side of my face.

And something soft bounced off my head.

I bolted up. Blinked my eyes. I heard everyone laughing.

I spotted the sponge chalkboard eraser on the floor next to me.

Mr. Ridgely stood at the front of the room, arms crossed, staring. "Sorry to wake you up, Vinny. Have a nice nap?" he asked.

I opened my mouth to answer—and yawned. Which made everyone laugh even more.

"Do you have the answer, Mr. Salvo?" Mr. Ridgely asked stiffly.

Everyone in the classroom grew silent. "Answer?" I chuckled nervously. I didn't even know what the question was.

I glanced at the chalkboard. There were numbers scrawled across it. We were doing math.

I peered over at Bobby for a clue. He shrugged his shoulders.

I was toast.

"Vinny, I'm waiting," Mr. Ridgely said, sneering. "The whole class is waiting. What is the answer?"

I gulped.

"Four?" I squeaked.

Mr. Ridgely's sneer faded from his face. "That is correct, Mr. Salvo. I apologize. I thought you weren't paying attention."

Whew! What a lucky guess.

When Mr. Ridgely turned back to the chalkboard, I glanced at Bobby again. He wiped his hand across his forehead and mouthed, "How did you do that?"

I didn't know how I did it—but I did know I wouldn't be that lucky again. Which definitely kept me awake for the rest of the morning.

An hour later a voice boomed over the loudspeaker system. It was our principal, Mr. Emerson.

"Attention, teachers and students. We will now all proceed to the auditorium for the Art Fair awards!"

"People, please make a double line," Mr. Ridgely ordered.

The class formed two lines and shuffled down the hall.

As I stepped into the auditorium, Sharon tapped me on the arm. I barely recognized her.

"What are you doing wearing a dress?" I asked. Sharon usually wears pants, and a vest with pockets. She says it makes her look like a real photographer.

"For the art awards today," she answered, tugging at her hem. "I wanted to look nice."

"Oh." I yawned. Sharon gabbed away about the awards. I nodded sleepily. Her voice sounded farther and farther away.

"Helloooo. Vinny, are you with me? *Hey, Vin! Wake up!*" My head snapped up. Sharon's nose was about an inch away from mine. She waved her fingers in my face.

"Uh. Sorry. What did you say?" I asked.

"What is with you today? It's like you're on another planet." Sharon stared into my eyes.

"I didn't sleep much, okay?" I grumbled.

She shrugged and pushed her hair back from her face. "Well, fine. But you don't have to be a major grouch about it."

"Do you mind?" Emily Nicholson shouted from a group of kids behind us. "You're blocking the door."

Sharon wrinkled her nose at Emily. Then she grabbed my arm and pulled me into the auditorium. "We need to sit near the front."

28

Sharon dragged me down the aisle, past the rows of worn leather seats. "I want to sit close to the stage. I'm sure my project is going to win."

I was sleepy. But not that sleepy. I locked my knees and screeched to a halt. *"Your* project!" I shouted. "Since when is it *your* project?"

"Try since always," Sharon said matter-of-factly. *"I* was the one who thought of doing a photo collage. *I* was the one who came up with the theme—neighborhood garbage.

"I was the one who took all the pictures," Sharon went on. *"I* was the one who developed them in my darkroom—"

"Oh, so *I* didn't do *anything?"* I cut in.

"All you did was glue them to the poster board and frame the picture." Sharon tried to drag me to a seat.

I glared at her. I wouldn't budge.

"Okay. Okay," she gave in. "I mean, *we* are going to win. All right?"

I gave her a "that's better" look and we sat down.

Mr. Emerson stepped up onstage and coughed into the microphone a few times. Then he started one of his long, long speeches. I closed my eyes and dozed off.

". . . And congratulations to all the students who entered this contest. Everyone did a great job!"

Mr. Emerson finished. He started clapping. Sharon nudged me in the side. I clapped too.

Then Ms. Young, our art teacher, took the stage to give out the awards. The kids she announced marched up to the stage. Ms. Young handed them each a ribbon and a certificate and Mr. Emerson shook everyone's hand. Then they lined up behind him. Big deal.

"In the photography category, the award goes to Sharon Lipp and Vinny Salvo," Ms. Young said.

Sharon jumped up from her seat and pumped her fist in the air. "Yes!"

She tugged on her dress and headed up the stage steps. I followed her, but I tripped on the last step and bumped into Mr. Emerson.

"Whoa, there," he said. He grabbed my sweater to keep me from falling off the stage.

The entire auditorium rocked with laughter.

My face felt hot—and I knew it was red. My head down, I followed Sharon as she marched to the podium.

"I thought we would get a trophy, at least," Sharon complained. We took our place at the far end of the line. "I worked so hard."

Before I could argue with her, Mr. Emerson said, "Smile, everyone."

Dustin Crowley, the school photographer, stepped up to take our picture for the school newspaper.

Dustin lifted the camera. "Uh-oh," he muttered. "I forgot to load the film. Um. Stay right there. Be right back." Then he raced out of the auditorium.

My eyes began to droop.

My glance fell to the floor—and I gulped.

Something was wrong.

Terribly wrong.

I saw shadows on the floor—six in all.

Six shadows—but only five winners onstage.

I counted the shadows again.

Definitely six.

My heart began to hammer in my chest as I stared at the sixth shadow. The one that didn't belong to anyone.

It shifted on the floor—changing into something that didn't look anything like a kid.

I tore my eyes away. Peered out into the audience.

I took a deep breath and tried not to glance down—but I did.

And gasped—as two twisted horns began to take shape. Then pointy teeth in an alligator snout. Big round eyes.

A thin body began to form. With long legs. And arms that ended in sharp claws!

I leaped back.

The shadow started to slide across the stage. Across the shadows of all the winners—heading straight for me.

7

I held my breath and watched the shadow monster slide past each of the award winners on the stage.

It stopped in the middle of the line—in front of Lindsay Holman.

"Stay there. Please," I whispered. "Just stay there."

It wavered in its spot. Then it began to move again.

I rubbed my palms on the sides of my jeans. I held my hands there, trying to steady my trembling legs.

What kind of creature is this? Is it really a monster? Is it dangerous? Why is it following me?

A million questions flooded my mind. But one kept repeating over and over. *What is it going to do next?*

I swallowed hard. The creature glided down the line. Snapping its terrifying jaw.

"Vinny! Look up!" Dustin had returned. "Okay, everyone, remember to smile!" he said as he loaded the camera with the film.

I glanced at the other kids in line. None of them seemed to notice the creature on the floor. They were all laughing and joking around.

The shadow slid closer.

It slinked past Sharon—and moved toward me.

I tried to run, but my feet wouldn't budge. I stood frozen—as the clawed hand stretched across the floor.

Stretching. Stretching. Reaching out for me.

It touched the toe of my sneaker. And an icy wave shot up through my veins. My whole body shook from the unbearable cold.

The claw moved up over my sneaker, inching up my calf. "My leg! It's numb! I can't feel my leg!" I shrieked.

My scream blasted over the microphone. Everyone in the auditorium stared at me.

I didn't care.

I leaped off the front of the stage. Dustin's camera flash went off, blinding me for a second with light. I landed on the kids sitting in the front row. They screamed and jumped up from their seats.

I ran for the exit. Dragging my numb leg. Glancing behind to see if the shadow was following.

But I couldn't tell where it was. All the kids had crowded into the aisle. Staring at me as I flew past them.

I flung open the doors of the auditorium with a *bang!*

I raced toward the double doors at the far end of the hall. Someone shouted behind me, but I didn't stop.

I crashed through the doors—and ran right into Ms. Grindly, the school nurse.

"Slow down!" she said softly. She gripped both of my shoulders.

"The monster!" I screamed. "It's coming! Let me go!"

"Where is it?" she asked calmly. "Where is the monster?"

"It's—it's . . ." I spun around to show her. But the monster wasn't there.

Ms. Grindly smiled at me. "See?" she said

soothingly. "No monster. Just your imagination. No monster at all."

"But I saw it!" I insisted. "In the auditorium!"

"I'm sure you did," Ms. Grindly said, patting me on the head. "Let's go to my office. And you can tell me all about it."

8

"Ms. Grindly thinks I'm nuts," I told Sharon and Bobby on the way home from school.

"The human mind *can* snap at any moment," Sharon replied.

"Thanks, Sharon," I said. "Thanks a lot."

"I can't believe they made you sit in the nurse's office all day. Why couldn't they just send you home early?" Bobby asked.

"Ms. Grindly wanted me to calm down. She made me draw pictures of the monster for her," I explained.

"Then did she believe you?" Bobby asked.

"No. I told you—she thinks I'm nuts," I said. "She just kept patting me on the head, telling me everything would be all right."

"Well, everything is not all right, Vinny," Sharon said. "You ruined the awards ceremony. And the winners' photograph. Dustin caught you in mid-air."

"How could I smile, Sharon?" I replied. "How could I—with that creature stalking me?"

"No one saw the creature, Vinny." She let out a sigh. "No one but you."

"But you *did* see it!" I exclaimed. "You saw that creepy shadow at my house. Remember?"

Sharon shrugged. "I saw your donkey shadow, Vinny. That's all. And your dad checked it out for us. It was nothing."

"Well, it's definitely something now. Something that's after me!" I shouted. Then I quickly shot a glance over my shoulder. Just to make sure IT wasn't there.

"I believe Vinny," Bobby said. "I believe there's a monster after him."

Now it was my turn to sigh. At least someone believed me.

"When did you first see this creature? What did it look like?" Bobby asked. "Those are the kinds of questions Detective Flynn always asks me."

Sharon pretended to gag, but I ignored her.

"I saw the monster for the first time in my room last night," I told him. "But I didn't get a

37

really good look at it. I-I was too scared to look at it."

Bobby nodded. "Go on," he said. He sounded like a detective.

"Today I got a real good look at it," I went on. "It has two twisted horns that snake out of the top of its head. And it has really sharp teeth—inside a long snapping jaw. And it has really sharp claws. I know they're sharp—because it tried to grab me in bed last night." I shuddered. "And it's kind of flat—just like a shadow."

"What happened after it tried to grab you?" Bobby asked, chewing a big wad of bubble gum intensely.

"It disappeared," I told him. "My mom flicked on my bedroom light and it disappeared. But it came back today in the assembly! And when it touched me I felt as cold as ice."

"A shadow monster?" Sharon said, giggling. "That's a good one."

Bobby flipped up the visor of his baseball cap. He blew a bubble and popped it loudly. "Yep, I've seen those."

"Really?" I asked with joy.

"Sure. They're big and green, right?" Bobby asked. He stuck his arms out straight and stiff—a Frankenstein pose.

"No," I said slowly. "They're just kind of gray. Like regular shadow color."

"Oh, right, right." Bobby nodded, chomping his bubble gum. "They're regular shadow color. But they've got these red glowing eyes."

"Uh. No. Just big round eyes. They didn't glow or anything," I said.

"Wrong monster, Bobby," Sharon said in her singsong voice.

"When you live on Fear Street, you see a lot of monsters," Bobby replied. "It's easy to get them mixed up."

We reached the corner where Bobby turned off. "See you tomorrow." He waved and headed home.

Sharon walked with me to my house, but she didn't come in. "Mom had to work only a half day today," she explained, standing on the curb in front of my yard. "I want to hurry home and show her my award." She clapped her hand over her mouth. "I mean, *our* award." She smiled.

Well, at least she was through being mad at me.

"Right." I waved at her as she walked away.

I went inside and dropped my backpack on the hall floor. "Mom? Dad?"

No one answered.

I walked into the kitchen. "Anybody home?" I called.

Still no answer. Then I spotted the note on the refrigerator. It said that Mom and Dad had gone shopping with Baby Joey.

"Great," I said, throwing up my arms in disgust.

I felt terrible. The whole school thought I was nuts, including my best friend. And Mom and Dad were gone. I was alone in the house.

I stomped to the kitchen cupboard where Dad hides his favorite brand of chips and swiped the bag. Then I grabbed a carton of milk from the refrigerator and took an extra-long swig. Right out of the carton.

I brought the chips and the milk into the living room and clicked on the TV with the remote.

"Talk show." *Click.* "Talk show." *Click.* "Talk show." *Click.* "Cartoons. At last." I flopped into a big overstuffed chair.

I tried to keep my mind on the show, but my eyes moved to the shadows in the room. They were growing bigger and longer as the sun started to set.

I sat up and slowly reached to the table for the chips bag.

I watched the shadows.

Each piece of furniture formed a strange one. But the couch cast the weirdest shadow of all. Big and lumpy.

I shoved a handful of chips into my mouth and nervously stared at the floor.

That lumpy shadow didn't seem right.

I stopped chewing.

The couch shadow shifted.

And changed.

Into a shape with twisted horns on top.

I shoved myself deep into the chair.

I stared in horror as the shadow formed itself.

I could see it more clearly now than ever. Its mouth gaped open with a double row of jagged, pointy teeth, like a killer alligator's. Its claws grew long and sharp.

Then the rest of its body quickly took shape.

I leaped up from the chair. Chips flew everywhere. I knocked over the carton of milk. It did a full flip, gushing all over the carpet.

I jumped over the mess and ran up the steps, two at a time.

My heart thumped in my chest.

I had to hide. But where?

I spun in a circle in the dimly lit upstairs hall, trying to think. *Shadows. What do I know about shadows?*

41

I snapped my fingers. They need light! You can't have a shadow without light.

The linen closet! It was big and dark. No windows. Perfect.

I dived for the closet, crawled inside, and yanked the door shut. Then I pulled my legs up under my chin in a tight ball. And listened.

What am I listening for? I thought. Shadows don't make sounds. Don't be stupid.

"But they're not supposed to form all by themselves, either. And chase you," I told myself. "The way this one did."

Listening didn't seem like such a dumb idea after all.

So I listened.

But all I heard was the pounding of my heart.

Then a terrible smell rose up. Surrounding me.

I inched away from the door—and bumped into a bucket. The diaper pail. Gross!

I pushed it away—and felt a tingling in my left hand.

I shook my hand—to wake it up. But the tingling feeling grew.

It moved up from my hand to my elbow. My fingers hung limp and numb. They felt—frozen!

"Oh, no!" I cried as the cold washed over my entire arm.

I glanced down at the crack under the door.
And saw it.
The shadow monster slinking underneath the door.
It must be creeping up my body.
Smothering me in its icy grip.

9

Wham!

I burst out of the closet and peered down at myself.

The shadow clung to me.

I jumped up and down wildly. Trying to shake it off. But it held fast. Slowly and steadily stretching up over my legs.

I stumbled down the stairs with the horrible black form stuck to me. Creeping up my chest. Freezing me.

"Get off!" I screamed as my arms started to go numb. "Leave me alone!"

I headed for the kitchen. But I could barely move. My legs had turned to two pillars of ice. Almost no feeling in them, and totally stiff.

I had to get help, but I couldn't even make it to the back door.

I staggered to the kitchen counter and held on to the sink.

No feeling in my fingers now. I couldn't hold on.

I crashed down on the hard tile floor.

I gaped in terror as the monster slid over my chest. My neck.

It's going for my head! I realized. It's going to freeze my brain!

"Get off!" I cried, trying to twist my body. "Let me go!"

The shadow inched up.

It crept over my chin.

"Nooooo!" I cried out in horror—my final scream as my lips turned to ice.

10

~~~

"**W**ell, look at old lazybones, lying on the floor," my mother sang out, stepping through the back door.

"What are you doing down there?" Dad asked.

"The sh-shadow—"

I glanced down at my body.

The monster was gone.

No dark shadow anywhere. Just the bright afternoon sun shining in from the open door.

"Vinny wants to make a shadow for you, Joey," Dad said, closing the door behind him.

"N-no! NO, I DON'T!" I shouted.

"Sadow!" Joey squealed. Mom carried him on one hip. He held a half-melted orange Popsicle in one hand. It dripped down his arm and was about to drip on me.

I rolled my head to one side to avoid the sticky orange goo. But I didn't get up. I didn't have the strength. I felt as if I had just run a triple marathon.

"No time for shadows," Mom said. "Vinny, please get up and help your father with the groceries." She made a big show of stepping over me.

"Oh, Mom," I groaned. "Do I have to? I'm kind of tired."

"What's the matter? Did you have a hard day at school?" Mom carried Joey to his high chair and strapped him in.

I nodded. "The worst."

She reached down and patted me on the head. "Well, wash up. We brought take-out Chinese food from the Golden Dragon. Let's eat while it's hot."

I slowly pulled myself to my feet. Up to the sink. I turned on the faucet and shoved my hands under the warm water. "Mmmm." The warm water felt good on my frozen fingers.

I guess I stood there for a while. Because the next thing I knew, Mom was turning off the faucet. "Vinny, I think your hands are clean enough." She handed me a towel. "Now sit down and eat."

Dad was already seated next to Joey. The food

from the Golden Dragon was steaming on platters in the center of the table.

One plate was full of brown noodles with green stuff and crushed peanuts sprinkled on top. The other had pieces of meat with orange glaze all over it.

"What is that stuff?" I asked, barely able to get my mouth to form the words.

"Sweet-and-sour pork, and noodles with spinach and peanuts." Mom picked up my plate and dished out a huge portion from each platter. Then she spooned some white rice into the middle.

I bent my head down to look at the food on my plate. It smelled great. But I couldn't make my hand reach for my fork.

I felt my head begin to nod.

My eyes begin to droop.

Then an icy slap hit the back of my neck—and everything went black.

"Vinny?"

I heard Mom's voice, but it sounded so far away. At the end of a long tunnel. She sounded as if she was sobbing as she called out my name.

"James!" she called to my father. "Do something! I can't."

I heard more sobs. Deep ones.

Poor Dad. He's crying, too, I thought. The shadow monster finally got me—and everyone is crying.

I slowly lifted my head, trying to focus on Mom and Dad.

They were doubled over at the kitchen table— with tears streaming down their faces.

Tears of laughter.

I stared at them laughing their heads off—and realized that I didn't feel the same cold numbness I'd felt when the monster attacked. Just the opposite. A warm stickiness dripped from my cheeks and chin. And smelled like—

"Peanuts and spinach," I moaned.

I realized the awful truth.

I had fallen asleep. Into the Chinese food. Face first.

A glob of spinach dripped from my cheek and landed in my plate with a loud plop. Another round of laughter from Mom, Dad, and Joey.

"You fell asleep in your dinner." Dad chuckled. "A perfect nosedive right into the noodles."

Mom wiped at her eyes. "I tried to wake you. I put a cold washcloth on your neck. Guess it didn't work!" she snorted. "Oh, that was"—she leaned forward and snorted again—"so funny!"

Joey gazed around the table at everyone. "Gahgin!" he cried. Then he slammed his face into his sweet-and-sour pork. Dad laughed so hard he almost fell out of his chair.

I wiped some peanut gunk off my chin with a napkin. I didn't think any of this was funny at all.

Mom glanced at me, forcing herself to be serious. "Vinny, why don't you clean up and go to bed? You must really be exhausted. I'll come up and check on you later."

I decided to do just that. I stumbled out of my chair. It clattered to the floor. The three of them doubled over in another fit of laughter.

"Funny. Real funny," I mumbled and left the room.

Upstairs, I washed the gunky spinach off my face and stumbled into my bedroom. But I couldn't bring myself to change into my pajamas.

I grabbed my flashlight and turned it on. Then I fell, exhausted, onto the bed in my clothes.

"I've got to find out what that monster is," I muttered as I drifted off. "And what it wants from me. Before it's too late."

I fell into a deep sleep. But when my alarm went off the next morning, I still felt exhausted.

"Vinny, you look gross," Sharon told me as we trudged home after school. It had rained all day. The sky was still gray, and puddles dotted the sidewalk.

I caught sight of myself in a car window as we walked past. Sharon was right. Huge purple circles rimmed my eyes. And my face was ghostly white.

I shuddered and looked back over my shoulder for the hundredth time—to make sure the creature wasn't following me.

"I wish Bobby were here. He knows all about monsters," I said. "He understands."

Mr. Ridgely caught Bobby drawing monster pictures during math—for the third time this week. So Bobby had to sit in detention after school.

Sharon clucked her tongue. "Bobby doesn't know anything. You know, there are people who study monsters. Important scientists. Not dumb kids like Bobby. Bobby is a big phony."

"Well, maybe he exaggerates a little," I muttered. "But his stories seem more real to me every day." I checked behind me once more.

"Like stories about shadow monsters?" Sharon rolled her eyes. "Are you guys in on this together? Are you trying to pull a joke on me? Is that it?"

I stopped walking. "Sharon, I am telling you the truth. And if you don't believe me, I don't think we can be friends."

Sharon stopped walking. "This shadow monster," she began. "What did you say it looked like?"

I sighed. "I told you, it has a big head and huge jaws with spiky teeth—"

"And big horns?" Sharon cut in. "Sort of curled—and really pointy?"

I swallowed hard. "Yeah. Why?"

"Because—" Sharon's voice was barely a whisper. "There's something that looks just like that. Over there." Sharon pointed over my shoulder.

I turned slowly. My stomach clenched into a huge knot.

There it was.

On the corner.

Standing.

I had never seen it stand up before. It rose at least six feet high on two shadowy legs. Its arms were long and thin and hung low. The horns on top of its head seemed to reach for the sky. And for the first time I saw that it had a tail. A menacing, spiked tail.

It moved swiftly—gliding more than walking. And it was coming our way.

My knees began to buckle. I tried to speak, but only a hoarse croak came out.

"Come on!" Sharon snapped. She grabbed the sleeve of my jacket and pulled me away. "Let's get out of here before that thing catches us!"

We ran across the nearest lawn. I glanced over my shoulder.

The shadow followed.

"What should we do? What should we do?" I shouted.

"Hide!" Sharon yanked me down behind a big, old car parked in the driveway.

We both hit the wet asphalt and froze. I squeezed my eyes shut.

I knew hiding here didn't make sense—

yesterday the creature found me in a locked closet. But I didn't know what else to do.

We waited. And waited.

We waited so long, the gray sky lightened and the puddles began to dry up.

Finally I peeked over the car. "It's gone," I announced in a whisper. "Maybe it didn't see us."

Sharon collapsed against the car's back tire and groaned. "That was so scary."

"*Now* do you believe me?" I demanded.

Sharon's head bobbed up and down. "I believe you. I believe you."

My legs trembled, but I managed to stand up.

Sharon yanked me back down behind the car. "What do you think you're doing?" she rasped. "Get down!"

"It's okay, Sharon. I told you, it's gone."

"Do you think it will come back?" she asked.

I leaned my head against the fender. "Probably. But I can't tell when. I spend all day looking over my shoulder, and I'm afraid to go to sleep at night."

"What do you think it wants?" Sharon asked, biting her lower lip.

I ran both hands through my hair. "I don't know what it wants," I replied. "But I don't think it will just go away. We've got to get rid of it."

Sharon crawled on her hands and knees to peer

around the side of the car. "Why do *we* have to get rid of it?" she asked. "It's after *you*, not me!"

"Because you are supposed to be my best friend!" I shouted.

"Uh—sorry. You're right. It's, um, just that I haven't read up on monsters yet. I don't really know much about them."

This was a first. Sharon admitting she didn't know something. "All you have to know is it's after me!" I told her. "And we have to find a way to stop it!"

"Okay, okay," she agreed.

She pulled herself up to her feet. She brushed the knees of her soggy chinos. Then she checked her camera to make sure she hadn't bumped it against the car. "So, what now?" she asked.

I took a deep breath. "We need to find out where that thing lives."

"How are we going to do that?" she demanded.

"Follow it," I said firmly.

"What?" Sharon gasped. "But we can't—"

"We *have* to," I cut in. "Then we have to find out exactly *what* it is. And get rid of it."

"I don't know. . . ." Sharon's voice trailed off.

My mind was made up. "Look, Sharon, you do what you want. I'm going after it."

Then I walked off, searching for the shadow monster.

I made my way down the sidewalk, peering under cars, behind bushes, everywhere.

"Hold it!" Sharon yelled. "You're not leaving me here alone! What if that monster comes back and gets me? Wait!" She jogged up and followed me.

"I don't like this," Sharon complained after we checked a few streets. "This is too scary. Let's go home."

"I can't, Sharon. I can't give up. Come on," I pleaded. "We have only one more street to check."

We turned the corner—and I spotted the shadow.

"There it is," I whispered. "It just crossed the street."

We crouched low and darted between the trees, keeping the hideous creature in sight.

"Why are we doing this?" Sharon wailed. "I don't want to do this. We could both get killed. I wish my mom were home. I'm going to call her. The first pay phone I see, I'm dialing and begging her to come get me."

"Sharon, be quiet!" I ordered.

My heart pounded away. I wanted to turn back, too. Run home, lock myself in my room, and dive under my covers with my flashlight.

But I knew I wouldn't be safe even then.

There was no place to run. No place to hide from this creature.

I took a deep breath and jumped behind the next tree.

At the corner I started to bolt across the street when Sharon grabbed the back of my jacket. "Vinny, wait!"

"Let go, Sharon!" I tried to push her hand away. "We'll lose it!"

But Sharon tugged harder. "Vinny!" she whispered. "Do you know where we are?"

I shook my head no.

With one shaky hand Sharon pointed up at the street sign.

I sucked in my breath.

Fear Street!

12

Almost every scary, creepy, weird thing that's ever happened in Shadyside happened on Fear Street. In the Fear Street cemetery. Or the haunted mansion. Or in one of the creepy old houses with the overgrown yards. Bobby swears to it.

I tried to forget about Bobby's terrifying stories as we inched our way past some deserted houses.

I kept reminding myself that the houses we were passing now were empty. But the hair on the back of my neck stood up. I couldn't shake the eerie feeling I was being watched.

Sharon must have felt it, too. She clutched my arm.

"Do you think the shadow monster lives in one of

these old places?" she whispered. "Bobby says they're filled with ghosts. He says he hears them groaning all night long."

"I thought you didn't believe Bobby's stories, Sharon."

"Well, maybe I do now," she replied. "Just a little."

A high-pitched cackle echoed from a boarded-up house.

Sharon grabbed my arm tighter.

"Just keep your eye on that shadow," I croaked.

I tailed the shadow around a curve—and gulped. Ahead of us sat the hulking shell of Fear Mansion. It cast an evil glow over everything that it surrounded.

Sharon stopped. "That's it," she declared. "I'm going home."

"No, you're not," I shot back. "We've come this far. That shadow is going to stop at one of the houses along this street. I'm sure of it. Then we'll know where it lives."

"And then we can go home and call Detective Flynn, and *he* can get rid of it," Sharon finished.

"Right." It sounded like a good plan to me.

But the shadow turned. It didn't stop at any of the houses. It leaped off the sidewalk and glided away. Sharon and I watched it disappear behind some dark, twisted trees.

I gasped.

"The woods. It's gone into the Fear Street Woods!"

We stared at the trees.

I knew Sharon was thinking the same thing I was.

Fear Street is a spooky, scary street. But when it comes to truly awful places—the Fear Street Woods wins first prize.

"Let's go home!" Sharon declared. "Now!"

"We can't," I told her. "We have to follow it."

"No way," Sharon said.

My hands began to tremble. I shoved them down into my pockets so Sharon wouldn't see.

"Yes, way," I insisted. "If you don't want to come, I'll go alone."

I felt my stomach turn a major flip-flop. I really didn't want to go without Sharon. But I couldn't let the shadow get away, either.

"Well, I'm not going to be stuck all alone on Fear Street!" Sharon squeaked. She glanced around nervously. "I guess I *have* to go with you."

"Okay, then. This way." I led Sharon between the houses—into the Fear Street Woods.

I held my breath as we walked slowly through the thick trees. Rough, scratchy vines hung from them,

60

blocking our way. They cut through our hands as we shoved them aside.

It was late afternoon. The sun hung low in the sky. But the leafy treetops blocked the sun out totally.

We were surrounded my darkness.

"Ow!" I banged my head on a low branch. "I wish we had a flashlight," I whispered.

"And an armored tank," Sharon added. She huddled so close to me she was practically walking on top of my sneakers.

A carpet of pine needles covered the floor of the woods. But it didn't have that fresh pine-cone smell. The air didn't smell at all.

Bobby always says that birds never sing in the Fear Street Woods—and he was right.

I didn't hear any birds. Or a squirrel, or a chipmunk, or any living thing.

It was totally quiet.

Too quiet.

"Do you see it?" Sharon whispered behind me.

I squinted in the darkness.

I slowly turned my head. Scanning the darkness. Searching between the gnarled trees.

I listened for a sound—the snap of a twig. Anything. But the woods remained still. Eerie silence.

"I don't see—"

Something sharp dug into my arm. Deep.

I whirled around.

"Sharon!" I cried. "What are you doing?"

Sharon pulled her fingernails out of my skin. "Let's call Detective Flynn now. I want to go home."

"But—"

A branch snapped—and our heads jerked in its direction.

"There!" I pointed ahead of me. "It's over there."

I ducked under a low branch. Leaped over a winding creek. Following the shady form as it led us further into the Fear Street Woods.

"The swamp monster," I murmured, remembering Bobby's story. My legs shook with every step. I could hear Sharon's raspy breathing behind me.

The air had suddenly turned icy cold, and I shivered.

Ahead, three huge gray boulders rose out of the ground, surrounding a tiny clearing.

"Wait!" I motioned to Sharon. "Look!"

The shadow monster stood in the center of the clearing.

"Don't move," I whispered. We both held our breath and froze.

The shadow turned its head from one side to the other. Searching the clearing. Then it disappeared behind the biggest boulder.

"That's it." I jabbed the air with one finger. "It must live behind that rock."

Sharon and I edged forward, quietly.

My pulse raced.

We slowly crept up to the big rock. Carefully I circled it. I reached the back—and gasped.

"Sharon!" I whispered. "We found it!"

Sharon inched forward. "Whoa!" Her jaw dropped open.

"A cave! It lives in a cave!" I exclaimed.

Sharon and I stared into the cave's huge opening.

Jagged points of crystal stalactites hung from the top. They glistened—even in the darkness.

And behind them glowed an eerie greenish-yellow light. A light that seemed to be shining from deep, deep inside.

Sharon grabbed hold of my arm.

With a terrible churning feeling in the pit of my stomach, I stepped into the mouth of the cave.

13

"**O**oooooh!" I moaned, clapping my hand over my nose. A horrible smell filled my nostrils.

Sharon started to gag.

I squinted into the cave. A narrow tunnel twisted and turned, heading downward. A the end of the tunnel the greenish light glowed brighter.

Following the sloping path, we made our way carefully toward the weird green light.

A heavy green mist began to swirl around our ankles.

I couldn't see my feet anymore.

We moved through the mist slowly, peering through the haze for the shadow monster.

The tunnel grew steep. I grabbed the sides of the cave walls so I wouldn't fly down. Warm, sticky slime coated the rocky sides. "Ewww." I let out a low moan.

My hands slid off the walls.

I tumbled down the tunnel.

And fell.

Into a huge hole filled with the slime—thick and bubbling and smelly.

The slimy ooze reached my waist. I struggled to jump out, but it sucked me down.

"Vinny!" Sharon cried. "Look!"

On the other side of the bubbling pool stood a kid about my height. He was wearing a long-sleeved red-and-white-striped T-shirt, jeans, and a baseball cap. His back was turned to us.

I tried to climb out of the disgusting slime again, but I slipped.

"Come on," Sharon ordered. "Stop fooling around in the pool. Let's go talk to the kid."

Then she lowered her hand and helped pull me out.

"Hello?" Sharon called softly, cupping her hands around her mouth. "Yoo-hoo."

The kid didn't budge.

"Maybe he didn't hear you," I said. "Let's get closer."

We circled the edge of the crater, holding our noses.

At the other side we saw that the kid's backpack

hung off his shoulder from a single strap. I spotted a notebook jutting out of the pack.

As we neared him, I could make out the words on the notebook. Waynesbridge Middle School—printed in red ink across the cover.

Waynesbridge was only a few miles from Shady-side. But I didn't know any kids from that school.

"Hey!" I called. "Over here!" I waved my hands to get his attention.

He didn't turn.

I jogged around him.

"Oh, no!" I staggered back against the cave wall.

The kid's arms were stuck out in front of him—as if he was trying to protect himself from something.

And his legs looked as if he was about to run.

But he wasn't running.

He was motionless—frozen in place.

I peered into his face.

His face! Eyes wide and staring. Mouth open in a silent scream. A face frozen like a statue's. Frozen with fear.

14

My heart pounded against my chest.

I waved my hand in front of the boy's eyes.

Nothing.

He didn't even blink.

He stood there—frozen in time.

Did the shadow monster do this to him?

I wasn't going to hang around to find out.

I turned and ran.

Sharon raced right behind me.

We charged past the bubbling pool. Through the cave's misty passage.

The horrible smell burned my eyes and lungs. I covered my nose and kept running.

We burst out of the cave and bolted through the

woods. The twisted branches scratched our faces and tore at our clothes.

We pounded down Fear Street. A sharp pain jabbed at my side. Sharon struggled for breath.

But we didn't stop running. Not until we reached my street.

I dashed up the lawn to my front door.

"Quick!" I gasped. I yanked open the door. "Get inside!"

Sharon and I stumbled into my house. I flipped the locks and bolted the front door. Then we ran around and locked the back door and all of the windows.

Nobody else was home. Dad and Mom had taken Joey to the doctor for a checkup. They wouldn't be back for a while.

"Did you see that kid's face?" Sharon panted as she followed me into the living room. She pushed her hair from her face and flopped down on the couch.

"I'll—I'll never forget it," I choked out, falling to the floor.

"Do you think he was—dead?" Sharon whispered.

"I-I don't know," I told her. "But I don't think so. He just looked—frozen. Like a statue or something."

"Maybe he wasn't real," Sharon said. "You know, maybe he was a dummy—like the kind in store windows?"

"No," I replied. "His face was too real for that."

Sharon shuddered. "Vinny, I'm scared. That shadow thing is dangerous. We have to tell someone."

"I know. I think you're right." I glanced nervously out the window. "Before it's too late. Let's call the police."

I jumped up from the floor and phoned from the kitchen. A deep voice answered on the first ring.

"Shadyside Police. Detective Flynn speaking."

I gave Sharon a thumbs-up sign. "Detective Flynn!" I shouted. "I-I have to report something—a monster."

"Calm down, son," the detective ordered. "Take a deep breath and tell me what's the matter."

"There's this kid," I said in a rush. "His body—at least. I don't know him, but I think he goes to Waynesbridge Middle School—"

"A body!" I heard the detective's chair squeak. I guessed he was sitting up and paying attention now. "Where's the body?"

"In a cave!" I cried. "In the Fear Street Woods."

"Where exactly is the cave?" Detective Flynn asked.

"It's about a ten-minute walk from the street." I

squeezed my eyes shut. Remembering exactly how we got to it. "You have to cross over a creek and pass some boulders. The entrance to the cave is behind the biggest boulder."

"Tell him about the glow," Sharon whispered from beside me.

"Oh. And there's this strange green glow that comes from inside the cave."

"Green glow? Hold on a second." I heard Flynn put his hand over the mouthpiece.

"Hey, guys! It's the Beasley kid," I heard his muffled voice.

"Not again!" I heard some moans in the background. "Hang up!"

They said a few more things I couldn't make out. Then there was a lot of laughter.

Detective Flynn cleared his throat. "Well, Bobby," he said into the receiver, "last week you told me there were vampires in the school gym. Do you think those bats have something to do with this cave? Maybe they live there."

I heard more laughter.

"Or maybe those huge ape-things that were flying around Fear Street you told me about last week live in this cave?" Detective Flynn added.

"I don't know anything about that. I'm not Bobby! And I really did see a kid's body. Because we were following this shadow. Well, not a shadow exactly. More of a monster—"

"Well, make up your mind, Bobby. Is it a shadow or a monster?" Detective Flynn cut in.

"It's a shadow that *turns* into a monster," I tried to explain.

"Wait," Detective Flynn said. "Let me write this down. Shadow. Turns into monster," he repeated very slowly. "Okay, go on. I'm sure there's more."

"It has really pointy horns and a big body—with a tail. And huge, sharp claws," I replied.

"Pointy horns, sharp claws," he mumbled. "Not as good as your usual stuff, Bobby," he added with a chuckle. "Sure you can't do any better than that?"

"This is for real!" I cried. "There is a shadow monster. Living in a cave in the Fear Street Woods. It's horrible—and it got that kid from Waynesbridge. I know it did. And now it's after me!"

"That's just terrible, Bobby," the detective said. "We'll check it out right away."

"He doesn't believe me," I told Sharon, covering the phone. "He thinks I'm Bobby."

"It was nice talking to you, Bobby," the detective continued. "Hey, guys. Say good-bye to Bobby."

Detective Flynn must have held up his phone because I could hear the other police officers loud and clear: " 'Bye, Bobby."

I hung up and looked at Sharon. "He doesn't believe us. He won't help us."

Sharon swallowed hard. "Then who will?"

"Nobody, Sharon. Nobody will believe us. We're on our own."

15

"It's all Bobby's fault," Sharon said with a groan. "If he didn't call the police every day with those stupid stories, Detective Flynn would have believed you."

"Forget Bobby. Forget Detective Flynn." I gnawed nervously on my thumbnail. "We have more important things to worry about. What if the shadow monster comes back? I have to be ready."

"A list," Sharon announced. "We need to make a list. You know, write down everything we know about the creature. Maybe that will help us figure out what to do."

"Good idea." I found some paper and a green felt-tip pen. "You write. I'll pace."

"Okay." Sharon plopped down at the dining table and began to write. "Let's see. The shadow seems to appear both at night and in the day."

"It needs light to be visible," I said, remembering how I'd seen it in my bedroom when the streetlight from outside shone into my room.

"Needs light," Sharon murmured.

Then I thought about the linen closet. I couldn't see it then. But I sure could feel it. A chill ran down my back.

"But it can be in a room that is completely dark," I told Sharon.

Sharon raised her head. "Anything else?"

"Let me think. . . ." I murmured.

It disappeared when Mom opened the kitchen door. And it also vanished when Mom came into my bedroom. There had to be a connection, but what? Mom? Was it afraid of my mother?

No. That couldn't be it.

"I got it!" I shouted. "When Mom came into my bedroom, she flicked on my light. When she opened the kitchen door, the sun shone in. That's when the shadow disappeared both times."

I stopped pacing.

"Bright light!" I cried. "It can't be in a room with really bright light. But I guess it can be outside or inside."

"Right, we saw it outside today. But the sun is bright. How come the shadow can be out in the sun?" Sharon asked, nibbling on the top of the marker.

That was a good question.

"I know! Because it was cloudy, remember?" I pointed out. "The sky was totally gray."

"Yes!" Sharon cheered. "That must be it. The light wasn't bright enough to keep it away." Sharon made some notes, then leaned back in her chair. "It got that kid in the cave and it's after you. But it's not after Joey or your mom and dad."

"Or you," I added. "It hasn't come to your house, has it?"

Sharon shivered. "Don't even say that."

"Now you know how I feel," I muttered.

"But why does it only want you? Why *not* me? Or Joey?"

I shrugged. I couldn't answer Sharon's question. I had no idea why the shadow monster kept coming after me.

I picked up Sharon's notes. "Let's see what we know. It wants me—for some reason. And it can get me in the dark and in dim light. Inside or outside."

Sharon sat forward. "But it can't get you in

75

bright light. So the only way to keep you safe is to keep you in bright light."

"That's it!" I shouted. "Follow me." I opened the door to the cellar stairs.

"Uh, Vin. I hate to tell you this, but your cellar isn't exactly bright."

"No, but there's lots of stuff down there that is!"

We dashed down the stairs. I headed right to Dad's storage space. "I'll fill my room with light!" I explained to Sharon as I held up a pair of large aluminum work lights.

I plugged them into the socket next to me. Blinding white light hit Sharon in the face.

"Hey!" she yelled. "Cut that out!"

I turned the lights off. "We can clip these to my headboard. They're like big headlights. Come on. Grab anything with a lightbulb."

I found an old table lamp, a night-light, the two work lights, and a couple of high-powered portable emergency lights.

Sharon grabbed a couple of long extension cords, a standing lamp, three big strings of Christmas lights, and the light-up plastic snowman we put in front of our house every Christmas.

Our arms full, we dragged everything to my room.

I hung the two big work lamps on either side of my headboard. I trimmed my entire mattress with the Christmas lights. I set up the plastic snowman on the floor next to my pillow. Then I positioned the other lamps all around the room. The floor became so crisscrossed with wires, I had to jump from one side of the room to the other.

Finally we turned everything on. The glaring blaze burned my eyes.

Sharon gasped. "It's like a night game at Wrigley Field," she said, shielding her eyes with one hand.

"Yeah." I squinted into the light. "It's awesome! Especially the blinking Christmas lights!"

I heard the rumble of a car engine and glanced out the bedroom window. I spotted my mom's minivan pulling into the driveway.

"Mom and Dad are home," I warned Sharon. "I don't want them to see what I'm doing. They'll think I'm nuts. I'm going to lock myself in my room."

"But won't they want you to come downstairs for dinner?"

"Tell them I feel sick," I said as I made a few final adjustments on the lamps. I wanted to make sure there wasn't a dim corner in the room.

"Okay," Sharon said, moving to the door. "But be careful. I'll call you tomorrow morning."

I heard the front door close as Sharon left. I quickly slipped into my pajamas. As I pulled back the covers on my bed, I heard a knock.

"Vinny, are you all right?" my mom asked from the other side of the door. "Sharon said you were ill."

I panicked. If Mom came in, she'd have a heart attack! "Um, just a minute. I'm doing my homework." I raced to the door, slipped into the hall, and pulled the door shut behind me. "I *am* feeling kind of sick," I explained. "I think I'll go to bed early."

Mom didn't have Joey hanging on to her. So she was really paying attention to me. Just when I needed her to be distracted.

She cupped her hand under my chin, tilting it up for a better look. "You *do* look tired," she murmured. "You've got big purple circles under your eyes." Mom pressed her palm against my forehead. "Are you warm?"

I moved her hand away from my face. "I'm fine. I just need to get some sleep."

"Well, okay." Mom studied me carefully. "If you still feel this way tomorrow, maybe we should think about keeping you home from school."

Great! Then I could stay in my room all day! I wouldn't have to worry about the shadow monster at all!

I was glad that Mom was so concerned about me.

But I didn't want to stand in the dim hallway any longer. Too dangerous. I had to get back into the light.

"Thanks, Mom. Don't worry. I'll probably be fine tomorrow."

I waited for Mom to go downstairs. Then I dashed back into my bedroom and locked my door.

I fell into bed, exhausted. I closed my eyes. I knew I was safe. The lights were protecting me. I should have fallen asleep instantly. But I didn't.

The lights were too bright.

I got up and rummaged through my dresser. I didn't find what I was looking for in the first drawer. Or the second. "Ah!" I found them in the third drawer. "My sunglasses."

I put them on and jumped back into bed. Perfect. I was sure I would fall asleep now.

I closed my eyes behind the sunglasses—but the frozen kid in the cave appeared in my mind. His terrified expression burned in my mind. I tossed and turned.

I rolled to my side and saw my radio.

"Maybe some boring talk show is on. That'll put me to sleep." I sat up and flicked it on.

ZZZZAAAP!

The sound crackled in my ears.

"Noooo!" I screamed. "This can't be happening!"

16

The room went black.

Every light in my room—snuffed out.

Even the plastic snowman.

I wasn't safe anymore.

"Oh, no!" I stumbled out of bed. "All those lights! I must have blown a fuse!"

I felt my pulse race double-time. With my arms stretched in front of me, I crashed blindly around my room.

What'll I do? What'll I do?

The shadow monster. It could be hiding *anywhere* now. Every second in the dark brought me closer to my worst nightmare.

I peeked into the hallway. All the lights were out there, too.

That means the whole house must be dark, I thought. So Dad will go down into the basement and fix the fuse.

Now, calm down! I ordered myself. The lights will come on any minute.

I waited in the dark.

No lights.

I broke out into a cold sweat.

The streetlight shone through the blinds. It left a striped pattern across the floor.

I stared at the stripes. Did one just move?

I blinked hard.

Yes. The thin stripes were twisting—merging into a larger shape.

"Hurry, Dad! Hurry!" My temples throbbed.

I groped desperately in my bed for my flashlight. I threw the covers and pillows on the floor. But I couldn't find it.

The shadow grew larger—forming into its hideous shape. The two twisted horns. The alligator jaw filled with the razor-sharp teeth! The claws!

The creature rose up from the floor.

It glided to my bed on its two long legs. Snapping its horrible jaws.

"No!" I cried out. I leaped onto the bed and pulled myself into a tiny ball against the headboard. "Dad!" I tried to scream, but my voice came out in a croak.

The monster crept closer and closer. It reached out a shadowy arm. Its claws raked my sheets.

I pressed my back hard against the headboard.

The creature hovered over me now. And I felt it—the awful numbing cold. Spreading up my legs. Up my chest. Through my arms. Piercing cold.

I held my hands in front of me.

"Leave me alone!" I cried. "Don't touch me!"

I shrank back, as far as I could. But the creature leaned forward and wrapped its hands around my neck.

The bitter cold swept up through my throat. Up into my head with a sharp sting.

"Go away!" I screamed. "Nooooo!"

17

Drip. Drip. Drip.

The faucet must be dripping in the bathroom, I thought drowsily.

No. Too loud, I realized. And echoing. More like water dripping in a basement.

Or a cave.

A cave.

My eyes popped open.

I was lying on the floor.

A greenish light flickered around me.

I took a deep breath and smelled that horrible smell.

Eerie shadows shifted across the rough stone walls.

"How did I get here?" I moaned.

I jumped up and nervously glanced around. I was in the chamber on the far side of the slime pool. That meant that the tunnel to the outside was on the other side.

I took a step forward—and tripped.

Over a body, sitting at my feet.

I shuddered.

That kid from Waynesbridge Middle School.

But something didn't look right.

He wasn't standing up. And he wasn't wearing the red-striped T-shirt we found him in.

He was wearing pajamas.

I kneeled down to get a better look at his face—and screamed.

The body on the floor—it wasn't the kid from Waynesbridge.

I stared at the most ghastly thing I had ever seen.

18

I shut my eyes.

I couldn't bear to look.

Then I took one more peek—at the face.

My face!

My *own* face stared back at me. Frozen in the same look of terror I saw on the boy from Waynesbridge Middle School.

No! This can't be real!

It has to be the most awful nightmare of my life.

Or the boy on the floor really isn't me.

That's it! It has to be someone else.

I gazed hard at the boy. He wore pajamas exactly

like mine. With the second button missing. And the yellow marker stain from Joey that Mom couldn't get out in the wash.

No! This is impossible! How can my body be down there and up here at the same time?

I squeezed my eyes closed and covered them with my hand. I'll count to three. When I open my eyes, I told myself, I'll be home, safe in my own bed.

"One. Two. Three."

I opened my eyes a tiny crack. Just enough to let in the creepy greenish light.

I opened them some more and sucked in my breath.

The dark shadow of a hand hovered in the air before me.

"Noooo!" I fell backward. "The shadow monster!"

I raised my other hand to protect my face.

Now I saw two shadow hands.

I wiggled my fingers. The shadows wiggled their fingers.

I waved my arms back and forth in front of my face. The shadows moved, too.

I struggled to breathe.

I glanced down at my body on the floor, hovering over it.

Hovering over what used to be me—and gasped in horror.

That wasn't me anymore.

Now I was only a dim gray outline.

I was a shadow.

19

~~~

This can't be happening. It can't be!

"Aiiiiii!" I cried. "A shadow! I'm a shadow."

I'll leave the cave, I thought. I'll escape. Once I get outside, everything will be okay.

I started to run.

And realized everything was not going to be okay.

Because I wasn't running.

I wasn't evening walking.

I was gliding. Gliding—just the way the shadow monster glided.

I whirled around—to search for a clue. Some way to turn back to the old me.

My eyes fell upon the boy on the floor—the boy who used to be me. His arms were stuck out in front. His hair was standing on end. And the look on his face! Pure terror.

My shadowy legs began to wobble. And the room began to spin. I started to sit down—when I heard the voices.

I hurried to the edge of the bubbling green pool and hid behind a big rock.

The voices grewer stronger. Closer.

I peered out from my hiding place. *Oh, no!* There stood the shadow monster. And other shadow monsters like it—dozens of them.

Some stood stooped over, twisted and deformed. Others rose up high, with knobby heads and spiky bodies—each one more hideous than the next.

I ducked down quickly and listened.

"Soon the sun will set," the horned shadow monster spoke. "Then we will go and gather energy."

The others let out a low humming sound. They slunk around the edge of the pool. I heard them drone, "Yes. Yes. Energy." Droning as if they were tired. So tired.

"Yes. Energy," the horned monster repeated. "Energy to live. Energy from children."

Energy? Energy from children?

Now it all made sense! Now I understood why *I* had been so tired. Why I couldn't stay awake in school. Why I fell into my Chinese food!

Each time the shadow monster touched me, it sucked the energy right out of me!

"The new one will join us tonight," the horned monster continued.

"I will not!" I jumped out from behind the rock. "I am not going anywhere with you."

The shadow monster faced me. It slithered close, snapping its menacing jaw. Baring its razor-sharp teeth. The others followed, surrounding me.

"You will come with us," the creature insisted. "You *are* one of us now."

"I am not!" I cried. "Why did you do this to me?" I pointed to my body—the one on the floor, wearing the pajamas.

"Because you created excellent shadows. You understand shadows. You like them."

"You're wrong!" I shouted. "I do *not* like shadows. I mean, I used to—but I don't anymore. I only made them for Joey."

"Well, it is too late," the horned shadow said. "You are one of us now."

"I don't want to be one of you! Change me back!" I shouted. "Change me back now!"

"You will not be changed back," the creature declared. "You are a shadow—forever."

20

A shadow forever!

I had to get home!

I had to find Mom and Dad. They would help me get my body back.

The monsters glided to the opening of the cave. They pulled me along.

I moved with them—pretending to be one of them.

The creatures floated out into the Fear Street Woods, filling the night sky with dark, shifting forms. Drifting off in different directions.

As soon as they were gone, I darted through the trees. I glided over the dried leaves, the gnarled tree roots that poked up from the ground. I checked behind me. Checking to make sure none of the creatures followed me.

With a final glance back, I slipped out of the woods and headed home.

I slid across my lawn. Mom's minivan and Dad's hatchback were parked in the driveway. Good, I thought. They're both home. I'll take them back to the cave with me. And they'll help me get my body back.

Then I saw the white police cruiser parked out front. Through the window I could see my parents talking to the officer.

Dad looked really worried. He waved his arms in big circles. He pointed up the stairs, then to the back door. Mom stood next to Dad, hugging Joey tightly. She dabbed at her nose with a tissue.

Oh, no! They think I'm lost, I thought, slinking up to the window. Poor Mom. Poor Dad.

I slipped through the crack in the front door. Into the living room. I stood in front of them.

"Mom! Dad!" I shouted. "I'm here. I'm okay! Look!"

They didn't hear me.

They couldn't even see me.

"Officer, I know my son," Dad said. "He wouldn't just disappear without a reason."

The officer nodded. He wrote something on his

pad. He was probably one of the cops who had laughed in the background when I talked to Detective Flynn.

"I know you're upset, Mr. Salvo. But Vinny's probably at a friend's house," the officer said. "He just forgot to tell you."

I yelled. I jumped up and down some more.

It was useless.

I was invisible to them. To everyone. Only the shadow monsters could see me. Hear me.

I have to show them I'm here. But how?

I glanced around the room. I could knock the lamp over, I thought. Make a crash. No, I realized. They would just think it fell.

The lamp!

I'll stand behind the lamp—then they'll see my shadow body on the wall.

"Yoo-hoo!" I yelled, jumping up and down in the lamplight. "Over here! Mom, please look!"

Mom glanced sideways. But she didn't see me. Her eyes were red-rimmed and glassy.

"Come *on*, Mom!" I kicked at the wall.

They had to notice me! They had to!

I tried once more, flapping my arms like a bird.

"Sadow!" Joey cried suddenly. His eyes grew wide. He pointed right at me. "Mama, sadow!"

"Yes! Joey!" I pumped my fist in the air. "Now they'll see me."

I threw my arms out to the side and hopped up and down. "I'm saved!"

"Sadow funny!" Joey squealed, clapping his hands together. "Look."

I held my breath waiting for them to turn around.

They didn't.

I jumped around some more.

Joey threw his head back and let loose with a big yell.

"Mama—*loooooooooook!*"

"Not now, Joey," Dad snapped, turning away from the police officer. "Carol, could you take him into the kitchen or something? I can't hear myself think."

Listen to Joey! Listen to him! You always do!

"Come on, Joey. Let's go into the kitchen for a cookie," Mom said.

"Sadow! Sadow!" Joey pointed to the wall and squealed.

"Joey, shhhh," Dad said, placing his finger to his lips.

"Binny! Sadow!" Joey screeched.

"A really big chocolate-chip cookie!" Mom said, carrying Joey off to the kitchen.

Joey drooled that long string of drool. It extended from his lower lip down the middle of Mom's back.

He pointed at me the entire way, screeching, "Binny! Sadow!"

Then he and Mom disappeared into the kitchen.

What am I going to do now? I moaned, drifting up to my room.

No one could hear me. No one could see me.

I'm doomed, I thought. The shadow monster was right. I'm going to be a shadow forever.

I made my way down the hall—and saw bursts of light flashing in my bedroom.

I glided to the doorway and peeked inside.

Sharon!

Sharon was in my bedroom snapping pictures like crazy.

"Oh, wow! You don't know how glad I am to see you!" I told her.

But, of course, Sharon didn't hear me.

"There has to be a clue somewhere," she muttered, raising her camera to one eye and aiming the lens at my bed. "People don't just vanish."

"That's right, Sharon!" I shouted. "I'm over here. Look!"

Sharon spun around—and focused on the window. *Click.*

Then she turned to face my closet. *Click.*

Sharon was doing a thorough job. As always.

She moved in a circle, shooting my room from every angle.

She turned and focused on the wall by my desk.

"This is it!" I thought. "I'm going to get Sharon to see me—right now!"

"Look at me!" I yelled, squeezing behind the desk lamp. "Look at my shadow on the wall!"

But she still didn't see me.

She placed her finger on the shutter button.

She pointed the camera right at me.

"Don't!" I screamed. "Don't take my picture!"

She focused the lens.

"Stop!" I cried out. "Don't point the flash at me. Too much light! Sharon, it's too much light!"

21

Click!

The light from the flash exploded in my face.

A hot, sharp pain shot through my entire body.

I collapsed on the floor.

Sharon pressed the button again. And another searing pain raced up and down my body. My body began to curl up. Shrivel.

"Stop! Sharon! Stop!" I cried out in agony. "You're destroying me!"

With all my strength I reached up and grabbed the edge of my desk. I slowly pulled myself up.

Sharon was about to take another picture.

I had to get her attention.

I glanced at my desk—and knew what to do!

I shoved my hands in front of the lamp.

I struggled to lace my fingers together.

I had only one chance at this. If Sharon clicked the shutter again, I'd shrivel up completely. I knew it. I had to get this right.

Sharon slowly raised the camera to one eye.

"Wait, Sharon!" I cried, my hands shaking in the light. "Just one second. *Please!*"

She focused the lens.

"Here it is! Look!" I made a perfect donkey shadow, with long ears and a hee-hawing mouth. Joey's donkey.

She reached out for the red button.

That's it, I thought. I'm toast.

I squeezed my eyes shut, waiting for the pain.

"Huh?" Sharon muttered.

I opened my eyes. Sharon lowered her camera. She tilted her head to one side as she studied my shadow.

"Yes! She sees it!" I cried. "Sharon! It's me, Vinny!"

Sharon stared at my donkey shadow. She squinted at it. "I must be seeing things," she muttered. She shook her head and turned away.

"Oh, no, you don't!" I raced in front of her. I hopped on the bed, waving my arms above my head. My shadow flickered on the wall above the headboard.

"Yipes!" Sharon cried, jumping back. Her face twisted in fear.

Oh, no! She must think I'm the shadow monster, I realized.

Before she could bolt for the door, I quickly clapped my hands together and made the donkey shadow again.

That stopped her. She peered at me again.

Then I made my shadow initials on the wall.

Sharon leaned forward and whispered, "Vinny?"

I nodded my head up and down, quickly.

"Is it really you? No, it can't be!" Sharon inched toward the wall.

"What happened to you? You're—you're a shadow. How did you do that? It's incredible!" Sharon said, fumbling with her camera. "I've got to get a picture!"

"No!" I jumped up and down, waving my hands back and forth above my head.

Sharon hesitated. "You don't want me to take your picture?"

I nodded very slowly and clearly. I had to make sure she understood.

"Why not?"

I mimed being shot in the chest. I staggered around the room. Then I fell backward and kicked my legs up in the air for extra effect. Then I lay on the floor, limp.

Sharon watched, eyes wide open. Finally she said, "You could *die?*"

I nodded yes.

"Whoa." Sharon put one hand to her head. "Vinny, this is too weird. What happened?"

I held my hands behind my head and opened my mouth as wide as I could. I snapped my jaw. Then I lurched toward her.

Sharon leaped back. "The shadow monster!" she cried. "The shadow monster did this to you? How?"

I tried different ways of telling Sharon that the monsters sucked energy from kids. But Sharon just shook her head. She didn't understand.

"Oh, Vinny. I'm sorry. I just don't get it."

I paced in a circle, trying to think of another way to tell her.

Sharon groaned. "I wish I could understand you. I wish I had taken a picture of the shadow monster. Then Detective Flynn would have believed you, and this would never have happened." She threw her camera on the bed. "I'm sorry, Vinny. I'm sorry I forgot to take a picture."

I stared at the shiny camera on the bed—and gasped.

Camera! That's it! I thought.

I jumped up and down to get Sharon's attention. "What, Vinny? What is it?" she shouted.

I waved for her to pick up the camera. And to follow me. I led her into Mom and Dad's bedroom.

I glided to Dad's dresser and pointed to the bottom drawer. I made a gesture for her to open it.

Sharon grabbed the drawer knobs and pulled. "What's in here, anyway?"

Dad kept his photography equipment in the lower drawer of his dresser, stashed beneath his boxer shorts. "Safer that way," he always told me. "Thieves will never look for expensive equipment in here."

"Eeew. It looks like your dad's underwear." Sharon wrinkled her nose as she peered into the drawer. "Do I have to touch it?"

I put one hand on my hip and jabbed hard with my finger at the underwear. Then I pretended I was lifting it up and setting it on the floor.

"Oh, all right." Sharon lifted the boxer shorts out of the drawer and tossed them on the floor. She spotted the camera gear right away.

"Cool!" Sharon whispered as she lifted the heavy camera. "This is a top-of-the-line single reflex camera with a telescopic zoom lens and a *mega* power grip flash unit."

"Yeah, whatever," I mumbled. But on the word *flash* I waved my arms wildly.

"Flash?" she repeated. "You want me to take this?"

I nodded. The little automatic flash from Sharon's instant camera hurt me. But maybe Dad's powerful flash unit could really do some damage to the shadow monsters. Destroy them—maybe.

I motioned to Sharon to follow me.

"Where are we going?" Sharon's face went pale. "Are we going to the cave?" her voice trembled.

I nodded yes.

"No way, Vinny." She set the flash down. "I'm really sorry. But there's no way I'm going back to the cave with you."

22

I spun around the room at full speed. I jumped up and down. I waved my arms madly. I chased Sharon around the room. I tried everything I could to let her know I was frantic!

She tried to leave.

But I blocked the door.

"Okay. Okay. Stop, Vinny," Sharon grumbled. "Get out of the doorway. I'll go with you. Just stop acting crazy."

I led the way down Fear Street to the Fear Street Woods, weaving in and out of the dim beam of Sharon's flashlight.

Sharon talked nonstop.

"I don't like this, Vinny. I don't like it one bit.

The only reason I'm following you is because you are my friend—and what happened to you could happen to me. And boy, would I hate that!"

What a friend! I thought.

I glided quickly through the woods.

I pointed ahead of me—to the cave entrance.

"I see it," Sharon said. "And I smell it!" She pinched her nose. "That stink is even worse than before."

We slipped inside, making our way through the green, swirling mist.

I led Sharon down the winding tunnel into the room with the bubbling crater full of green slime. A green cloud hovered above the pit. Part of it stretched toward us.

Sharon started to choke from the smell.

She stopped. "I can't do it. I can't go any farther."

"Come on, Sharon," I pleaded silently to her. "I need your help."

"Vinny, I'm so scared. I can't even move."

I understood. I felt the same way. But I couldn't tell her that.

Sharon's shoulders sagged. "Okay. Okay." She covered her nose with her hand. She stared at me. "I'll keep going."

The two of us slowly inched around the bubbling

pit. When we reached the other side, we ducked into the next chamber.

I rushed forward, ready to show her my body. Ready to figure out how to get back inside it!

But the chamber was empty.

"My body!" I cried. "My body! It's gone!"

I glided out of the chamber. Back around the bubbling pit. I shot down the tunnel, all the way to the cave entrance. Searching. Searching.

But there was no sign of my body. Anywhere.

23

"**W**hat is it, Vinny? What are you looking for?" Sharon asked. Her voice trembled.

I slapped my hands against my shadowy form over and over again.

"Your body," she murmured. "Ooooh," she moaned softly.

Sharon flashed her light around the cave. Her light fell upon a dull green glow, shining from way back in the cave.

"Let's check back there." She pointed to the eerie light.

I followed Sharon through a narrow, twisting tunnel.

"It's another chamber," she announced as we reached the end of the winding passageway.

We approached the room.

The greenish light—no longer a dim glow. It shone brightly, outlining the entrance.

Sharon inched forward slowly.

Then she stepped into the room—and screamed.

Screamed at the five bodies standing there.

Bodies of kids—frozen in hideous terror. Their mouths hung open, crying out. Their eyes, wide with fear.

"Vinny!" Sharon gasped. "Ugh! I can't look!" She moaned and covered her face with her hands.

I didn't want to look, either. But I couldn't tear my eyes away.

A boy was bending on one knee. His hands still held the shoelace he must have been tying—just as a shadow monster froze him. His face, twisted in pain.

A girl had one leg lifted up behind her. One arm stuck out in front of her. Her head turned back over her shoulder. Her mouth open, in a silent scream of terror.

The other bodies stood behind them. I couldn't see them clearly. But they all appeared the same. Statues frozen in time.

But the worst part was the slime.

Each body was sealed in a layer of green slime.

Just like the ooze in the cave's crater. It covered them like giant transparent pods.

Sharon brushed against one of the slimy bodies.

"Ugh!" she shrieked. "I touched one. My shoulder touched it. It's so gross!" She bolted for the chamber opening, wiping at her arm. "I have to wash my arm. I have to get it off me!"

"No!" I hurled myself in front of her. "We can't leave yet."

"Get out of my way, Vinny," she demanded. "I'm leaving. There's no reason to stay. Your body isn't here."

Not here!

I swooped over to the bodies.

Stared into their tortured faces.

Faces I didn't recognize. None of these other kids were from Shadyside. The monsters must have taken them from some other places.

But my body! Where was it?

I have to be here. All these kids are here. I should be, too.

But I wasn't.

I fell back against the cave wall.

I'm going to be a shadow forever—

"L-look." Sharon stared past me. To a narrow crevice in the wall at the far side of the room.

"That's me!" I ran for my body, encased in the same green pod as the others.

"Vinny!" Sharon turned her face away. "Oh, I can't bear to look at you. I'm going to gag."

I wanted to gag, too.

My body was sealed in the green slime—covered from head to foot.

It was disgusting.

But I had to get back inside it—no matter what.

I stepped back.

Then I charged at my body with all the strength I had—trying to leap back in.

I bounced off the slimy pod and hit the floor.

I tried again.

Crashed to the floor again.

"Sharon, help me!" I cried. "What should I do?"

Sharon watched me fall to the floor and groaned.

"It didn't work. You need to try something else!"

"What?" I shouted. I waved my arms at her, making big question marks in the air. "What can I do?"

"We have to get the slime off," Sharon said. "Maybe you can jump back in then."

I nodded in agreement.

We stared at each other.

Sharon didn't move.

"Oh, no!" she cried. "Don't look at me. I'm not touching that stuff."

I glided over to Sharon and loomed over her. I snapped my jaw at her.

"Stop it, Vinny." She leaped back. "I'm going to do it—I, uh, was just kidding."

Sharon slowly moved to my body. She dug her fingers into the slime that covered my chest. "Ewwww!" she shrieked. "This stuff is gross. And it really stinks. I think I'm going to puke." She backed away.

I loomed over her again.

"Okay, okay," she said, digging her nails in.

She peeled away a chunk of the slimy wall that held my body. Green ooze seeped out of the hole. It dripped down Sharon's hand. Her leg. Onto her sneaker.

Her face twisted in disgust. She clenched her teeth and continued to work.

She dropped the pieces as she peeled away.

They landed on the floor with a tinkling sound, like shattered bits of glass.

Ooze seeped out of every opening she made, puddling on the floor around her.

Sharon finally peeled the last piece of the slimy pod from my body.

"There. You look like yourself again," she declared. "If your eyes weren't stuck open, you'd look as if you were still asleep in your room."

Yeah, right, I thought. My body still wore the blue-and-white-striped pajamas with the missing button. But my face didn't look as if I were asleep.

It looked totally terrified.

"Okay, Vin. Try it again," Sharon said.

I stepped back.

What if this doesn't work? Then what am I going to do?

"Come on, Vin!" Sharon yelled at me. "What are you waiting for?"

I took a deep breath.

Then, with one mighty leap, I hurled myself at my body.

24

"**Y**eeeaaaaaa!" I screamed at the top of my lungs.

My hands flew up to my face.

My hands. *My* face.

Not shadows.

I glanced down at my body. I was wearing blue-and-white pajamas. I was really me again!

"It worked! I'm back inside!" I cheered. I wiggled my fingers in front of Sharon's nose.

"Yes!" Sharon cried. "I knew I could do it!"

I shot her an annoyed glance.

"Uh, sorry. I knew *we* could do it," she said.

I danced in front of Sharon, kicking my legs and flapping my arms. "I'm back! I'm back! I'm back!" I shouted with glee.

And then I froze.

What was that sound?

Sharon heard it, too. A whooshing sound. We both jerked our heads toward the tunnel entrance.

"The shadows! They're back!" I whispered.

Sharon's eyes grew huge.

"We can't let them find us!" I groped desperately along the walls of the chamber, searching for an opening. "We have to find another way out."

Sharon searched, too. "It's no use, Vinny!" Sharon cried. "We're trapped."

"No!" I declared. "We'll just have to sneak out— the way we came in."

We charged through the narrow passageway, into the chamber with the crater of bubbling ooze.

Through the thick green mist, I spied the terrible horned shadow monster. It slowly crept alongside the slime pool. Sharon and I ducked behind a boulder.

We peered over it, watching the creature slink next to the pool. Tossing its hideous head from side to side.

It snapped its jaws. Baring its double row of sharp, jagged teeth.

The other shadows drifted into the cave. Following the horned one. Snapping their jaws.

Sharon gasped—loudly.

The shadow monster whirled to face us.

We ducked behind the boulder—too late.

It saw us.

The creature glided toward us—swiftly now.

I broke out into a cold sweat. Sharon trembled beside me. "DO SOMETHING, VINNY!" she wailed.

I grabbed Dad's flashgun from Sharon's pocket.

The shadows crept closer.

I pushed the Power switch.

"Hurry, Vinny!" Sharon cried. They're coming!"

I glanced up. The shadow monster stood steps away. It arms outstretched, ready to grab us.

"Come on! Come on already!" I clutched the flash tightly and shouted, waiting for the Ready light to blink on.

The shadow reached out with its claw. Reached out and touched my shoulder.

A sharp, cold pain shot through me.

I stumbled backward.

I dropped the flash.

I grabbed for it, but my fingers were numb—frozen.

"Sharon, the flash!" I screamed.

Sharon stared at me, terrified.

She didn't move.

The creature lunged forward. Its claw stretched out—aiming for my throat.

I dropped to the floor.

Snatched up the flashgun—and fired.

25

Z zzz-zap! Zzzz-zap!

An electric crackle filled the air as a flash of brilliant white light flooded the cave.

I pumped the flash trigger, sending out bursts of the blinding light.

The monsters jerked back.

Moaning. Rocking from side to side.

Their heads twisted in pain. Their long, hideous tails beating the cave floor.

"It's working, Vinny!" Sharon shouted, clicking her camera to set off her flash.

The monsters opened their mouths in silent screams. They began to curl up. Shrink and shrivel. Growing smaller and smaller.

I hit the flash trigger again and again, hitting them all with the blinding light.

They shrank back. Wrinkled up.

Their jaws snapped madly as the light destroyed them.

And they withered away.

All that remained was a pile of blackened ash where they once stood.

"Let's get out of here!" I cried.

I grabbed Sharon's hand, and we bolted for the mouth of the cave.

Sharon stiffened and skidded to a stop.

I pulled hard on her arm.

"Run!" I yelled, turning to face her. "Don't stop! Run!"

"We-we can't," she stammered, pointing up ahead.

I jerked around—and saw them.

More dark shadows. Hovering in the entrance to the cave.

Blocking our way.

26

"**V**-Vinny. What should we do?" Sharon croaked.

"Help them," I replied.

"Huh?"

"We have to help them, Sharon," I said. "Look. There are five of them. These shadows belong to the bodies in the back of the cave!"

"You're right!" Sharon exclaimed.

I motioned for the shadows to follow us to their bodies.

"I hope they realize we're their friends," I whispered to Sharon as the shadows drifted closely behind us.

Sharon shot a nervous glance over her shoulder. "Maybe we should, um, make a run for it."

"No! We have to help them," I insisted.

"I know. I know. I was just kidding." Sharon gulped.

Sharon and I worked fast. We peeled the pod layers of slime off the bodies. Green slime oozed out and puddled up on the floor, seeping over my bedroom slippers. But I continued to rip away the horrible stuff.

The shadows hovered over us. Watching us.

Finally we were done, but the shadows just gazed at us. They didn't move.

"Why are they st-staring at us?" Sharon stammered.

"I don't know," I answered, puzzled.

"Well, I wish they would stop," Sharon said. "They're giving me the creeps."

"Hey! I've got it! I bet they don't know what to do. We have to act it out for them!" I exclaimed.

We did—and the five shadows ran, full-speed, into their waiting bodies.

It worked!

The kids jumped up and down, shouting with joy.

"Let's get out of here!" the boy from Waynesbridge yelled and took off.

We all charged after him.
We ran through the horrible cave.
Out into the Fear Street Woods.
And headed home.

27

A week later it was hard to believe Sharon and I had ever battled the shadow monsters.

My parents were so relieved to see me—until I told them what had happened.

They didn't believe me. They said I made the whole thing up—because I forgot to leave them a note. Sharon backed me up, but they didn't believe her, either. So they grounded me for two weeks.

On Friday night I had to baby-sit Joey. I asked Sharon and Bobby to hang out with me.

We made popcorn. I put Joey in his playpen. Then Bobby asked us to tell him about our entire adventure—again. We'd already told it to him about ten times. But Sharon was more than willing.

"Vinny and I were trapped in the monsters' cave," she said in a dramatic whisper. "We were armed with only my camera and Mr. Salvo's flash-gun. You should have seen us, Bobby. We destroyed them. All of them! It was awesome."

"Now I remember," Bobby said, scooping up a handful of popcorn from the bowl. He tossed the bits of popcorn into his mouth, one by one. "I've seen that cave. I know the shadow monsters you're talking about. I've seen them."

"You have?" I asked in amazement.

"Oh, sure." Bobby waved one hand around. "Aren't they big and black, like bats?"

"Bats?" Sharon repeated, frowning at me.

Bobby spread his arms out to the sides. "Big vampire bats. With long creepy fangs. During the day they travel as shadows and live in a cave. But at night they turn into bats. Am I right?"

Sharon rolled her eyes. "Yeah, you're right, Bobby."

Bobby leaned back against the couch with a shrug. "See? I told you I know everything there is to know about creepy things that happen in Shady-side."

The mantel clock in the living room chimed nine times. "Nine o'clock!" Bobby leaped to his feet. "I have to get home. Mom doesn't like me walking on Fear Street after dark."

Bobby left and Joey started squealing. "Sadow, Binny! Sadow!"

"No shadows," I said firmly. "Not tonight. Not ever again."

Sharon agreed. "Why don't we put on a video?"

While Sharon and I sorted through the stack of videotapes by the TV, I could hear Joey giggling behind us.

"Dat funny!" he squealed. "Gah-gin!"

Sharon and I turned—and gasped.

Right above Joey's playpen, outlined clearly on the living room wall, we both saw the shadow.

The unmistakable shadow of a donkey.

THE BUGMAN
LIVES!

1

"Hey, Janet! Want to see me jump the curb?" Carl Beemer *whooshed* past me on his Rollerblades.

I didn't look up from my weeding. I didn't want to watch Carl jump the curb. I didn't want to watch him do anything—except skate away.

Carl is a pain. All he does is brag, brag, brag.

Carl zoomed up the front walk and stopped next to me. "Having fun?" he taunted.

Ignore him, I told myself. Maybe he'll leave. I kept working on the flower bed. Jabbing at the dirt and pulling out the weeds.

1

"I bet you aren't getting paid for that, are you?" Carl asked.

I wasn't. Mom says weeding is part of my family responsibilities. But Carl didn't have to know that. "None of your business," I muttered.

Carl laughed. "You aren't," he guessed.

I felt my face get hot. I hate it when Carl is right.

Carl stuck one of his big feet in front of me. "See my new Rollerblades? Cool, huh? I paid for them myself. I'm making big bucks with my mowing business."

I sat back in the grass and stared up at him. "Really? Maybe I'll get some jobs, too." If Carl could make money mowing lawns, I knew I could. I can do anything Carl can do—except better.

"Yeah, right," Carl answered. "Who would hire you?"

"Lots of people," I shot back. "By the end of the week I'll have more jobs than you do."

"No way!" Carl protested.

"Remember the recycling contest at school?" I asked. "I brought in eighteen more pounds of paper than you did."

Carl snorted. He sounds like a hog when he does that. "If I knew old telephone books counted, I would have beat you."

"Janet," Mom called from the house. "Are you getting those flower beds weeded?"

2

"Almost done!" I yelled back.

Carl snickered. "Yeah, Janet. Just think of all the money you're making doing that weeding." He skated off.

I rocked forward onto my knees again and started yanking up the weeds as fast as I could. I had to find some mowing jobs right away. I wanted *twice* as many as Carl had.

If I earned enough money, maybe I could go to camp next year like my friends. Then I wouldn't have to spend another summer in Shadyside with only Carl Beemer for company.

I scooped up all the weeds and stuffed them in a big plastic bag. "Mom!" I yelled. "I'm done. I'm going for a walk, okay?"

"See you later," she called.

I rushed over to our next-door neighbor's house. I combed my short, curly brown hair with my fingers and brushed the dirt off my shorts. Then I rang the bell.

Mrs. Kemp opened the door and peered at me through the screen.

"Hi, Mrs. Kemp," I said. "Do you need someone to mow your lawn this summer? I'm a good mower."

Mrs. Kemp smiled. "Sorry, Janet. I have a lawn service that does all my yard work."

"Oh," I said, feeling disappointed. "Well, thanks

3

anyway." I hurried back to the sidewalk. At least Carl didn't see that, I thought.

Then I heard him laughing. Carl popped out from behind the big oak tree in Mrs. Kemp's yard. "I'm a good mower," he squeaked in a high little voice.

"I don't sound like that!" I exclaimed.

"I don't sound like that!" Carl squeaked.

I stomped over to the next house. I heard the *shoop shoop* of Carl's skates behind me.

Why isn't Carl at camp this summer like Anita and Sara? I thought. Or at the Grand Canyon with his family like my best friend, Megan? Or visiting his grandmother like Toad?

Why does he have to be the one kid in the neighborhood—besides me—who is stuck spending the summer in Shadyside?

I rushed up to the Hoffmans' door. They didn't need their lawn mowed, either. And neither did the Hasslers, the Martins, or the Prescotts.

But I refused to give up. Especially with Carl watching.

I trooped through the neighborhood trying every house. Everyone told me they mowed their own lawn or they had already hired someone.

One guy had already hired *Carl.* Of course, Carl didn't bother to tell me that before I went to the door and asked. The jerk.

4

"You're striking out big time," Carl informed me. "You can't get a job anywhere!"

It took all my strength to keep from turning around and knocking his head off. "Why do you keep following me?" I demanded. "Go away. Get a life."

But he stayed right behind me. Of course. Carl never did anything I wanted him to.

I turned the corner—and heard Carl give a big gasp.

"*Ooooo*—Fear Street!" he teased. I glanced back at him. He had both his hands stuffed in his mouth, pretending to bite off all his fingernails.

Carl thinks he is hilarious. I shook my head as I started toward the first house.

This place definitely needs my help, I thought. High grass covered most of the crooked stone walkway. Weeds were taking over the flower beds. And dark green ivy clung to the porch railing and the front of the house.

I climbed the porch steps and rang the bell. A woman about my mom's age opened the door. She had short black hair, and she looked friendly.

"Hi," I said. "My name is Janet Monroe. I wondered if you need someone to mow your lawn this summer."

She smiled. I noticed she had a little gap between

5

her top two teeth. "That would be wonderful. I've been looking in the paper for someone to help me with the yard. Your timing is perfect."

"Fantastic!" I exclaimed.

"I'm Iris Lowy," the woman said. "When can you start, Janet? As you can see, my yard needs a *lot* of work." We both laughed.

"I can start right now," I told her.

"Great. How much do you charge?"

"Umm, four-fifty an hour," I said. I hoped that was okay. I hadn't thought about how much to ask for.

"Sounds fair," Mrs. Lowy answered. "The lawn mower is in the garage." She pointed around to the side of the house.

"Thanks," I said. As soon as she closed the door, I turned and grinned at Carl.

"So you got one lousy job," Carl taunted. "Big deal." He skated off down the street.

Finally, I thought. At least he isn't hanging around to watch me work.

I trotted up to the garage and wheeled out the mower. An old gas one. The kind you have to start by pulling a cord.

I hauled it through a wooden gate and into the side yard. I sighed as I gazed at the long strip of overgrown grass.

6

You wanted a job, I reminded myself. I yanked on the pull cord. Nothing.

I gave the cord another yank. Nothing.

"Come on, come on," I muttered.

I jerked the cord again. The motor blasted into action. The vibration raced up my hands and through my body.

I leaned my weight into the mower and pushed. I could feel the muscles in the backs of my legs strain as I struggled across the side yard.

The air was so heavy and hot I could hardly breathe. Sweat slid down my back. It trickled down my forehead and dripped into my eyes.

I knew Carl would love it if I quit, so I pictured him watching me with a stupid grin on his face. That helped me keep mowing.

My palms burned and itched against the handle of the mower. By the time I finished the side yard, I could feel blisters forming on both of them. And my hands are pretty tough.

I stopped the mower, letting the engine idle. I wiped my face on my sleeve and took in a deep breath. I love the smell of freshly cut grass.

I shook my arms out at my sides. My muscles already felt sore—and I had barely started.

I rolled the mower around to the backyard.

That's when I saw it.

A huge, tangled mass of tall weeds and grass in the far corner of the yard.

The rectangle-shaped patch wasn't that big—it looked about the size of the rug we have in our front hallway. But some of the weeds grew higher than my waist.

I should get it over with, I decided. I dragged the mower over to the patch.

Hundreds of tiny black bugs buzzed in the grass. And some of the weeds looked really prickly.

You can do it, I told myself. I aimed the mower at the patch and shoved as hard as I could.

The grass tangled around my knees. Thistles scratched my legs. I could feel the little bugs crawling over my bare skin.

Wheer! The mower squealed as I forced it through the patch. My muscles trembled with the effort.

The scream of the mower grew louder and louder. I didn't think I could stand another second of it. I wanted to cover my ears.

I slammed myself against the mower. Giving it one last huge shove.

Crack!

The mower bashed into something.

The motor groaned to a stop.

What happened? What made that horrible cracking sound?

I pulled the mower back and crouched down. I

8

shoved the grass back with my hands and found a stone.

A large, flat stone.

I ran my fingers over it. It felt icy cold. And smooth.

Then I felt deep grooves. I pushed more grass out of the way. And I saw the word HERE chiseled into the stone.

I yanked away clumps of weeds with both hands until I uncovered the whole stone.

It was one of the hottest days of the summer—but a cold shiver ran up my back when I read the words carved there.

HERE LIES THE BUGMAN. WOE TO ANYONE WHO WAKES HIM.

2

I jumped up.

A tombstone? I thought. Someone is *buried* under there. I'm standing on a grave.

I backed away. My feet got tangled in the weeds and I hit the ground hard.

I could feel weeds poking into my back. A swarm of tiny black gnats hovered above my face.

I'm on a grave, I thought.

I fell right on top of a grave. My heart thudded. I scrambled to my feet. And looked down.

HERE LIES THE BUGMAN. WOE TO ANYONE WHO WAKES HIM.

Right through the stone was a big jagged crack. A crack I made.

I turned and ran to Mrs. Lowy's back door. I pounded on it.

Mrs. Lowy jerked the door open. "Janet, what happened?" she asked. "Are you hurt?"

"I think I ran over a tombstone with the mower and broke it," I said. All my words ran together.

"What?" Mrs. Lowy cried. "A tombstone?"

I pulled in a deep breath and tried to talk more slowly. "I was mowing that overgrown patch in the side over there and I hit something. I think it's a tombstone."

"It can't be," Mrs. Lowy said. "Show me."

"Okay." I led the way back over to the stone and pointed down at it. My hand was shaking.

"My, my," Mrs. Lowy said. "I would have been scared if I found that, too. But it has to be a joke. Some teenagers probably heard those old stories about the Bugman and thought it would be funny."

"What stories?" I asked.

"Oh, you know. Stories about the man who used to live in the house next door years and years ago," she told me.

I shook my head. I still didn't know what she was talking about.

"Everyone called him the Bugman. He was fascinated by bugs and spent all his time studying them,"

Mrs. Lowy continued. "He was odd—didn't go out much or talk to his neighbors. People said he eventually turned into a bug himself."

"That's creepy." I wrapped my arms tightly around myself.

"Well, you know how everyone likes to tell stories about Fear Street," Mrs. Lowy said. "I'm sure someone put that stone there as a prank. I've never seen it before. And I've lived here for five years."

I nodded and tried to smile. I didn't want Mrs. Lowy to think I was a baby.

"Don't bother to finish that spot," Mrs. Lowy said. "It's not part of my yard anyway. It belongs to the house next door. Whoever ends up buying the house can deal with it."

"You mean no one lives there?" I glanced over at the other house. It was in worse shape than Mrs. Lowy's.

"It's been empty for years. I wish someone would take it. It would be nice to have neighbors." Mrs. Lowy sighed. "Do you want a Coke or anything before you go back to work?" she asked.

"No, thanks," I told her. I wanted to get out of there—fast.

"If you change your mind, let me know," Mrs. Lowy called as she headed back to the house.

I grabbed the mower handle. I ignored the blisters

on my hands, my sore arms and legs, and the heat. All I cared about was finishing the job so I could leave. I turned the mower around and went back to work.

But I couldn't stop thinking about the tombstone. The word *Bugman* pounded in my head with every step.

Bugman.

Bugman.

Bugman.

"Come on, Janet," I said to myself. "Chill out." I decided to check the tombstone. Maybe it wasn't as bad as I thought.

I left the mower running and rushed over to the stone. The huge crack was still there. The stone was split in half.

I read the words again. HERE LIES THE BUGMAN. WOE TO ANYONE WHO WAKES HIM.

What if I did wake him? What if he climbed out of his grave? What if he's watching me right now? What if—

Stop it, I ordered myself. I marched back over to the mower. Mrs. Lowy is right. The tombstone is just a stupid joke.

I glanced at it over my shoulder. Nothing.

I pushed the mower a little farther. Then I looked back at the tombstone again. Nothing.

It's going to take all day if I keep stopping to make sure the Bugman isn't coming out of his tomb! I thought.

"So you finally finished," Carl called. "Took you long enough." He jumped out of the cedar tree in my front yard and landed right in front of me.

I groaned. "Carl, don't you have a home?"

"Mowing is hard work. I bet you're ready to quit. If they want you to do the lawn again, you can give them my number," Carl volunteered.

"No way!" I plopped down on the grass and picked off some of the thistles stuck to my shorts. "Mrs. Lowy already hired me for the rest of the summer. She wants me to weed and water, too."

Carl sat down with his back against the tree trunk. "How did you get all those little cuts?"

Talking to Carl is better than talking to nobody, I decided. A little better.

"One spot in the backyard had all this high grass and weeds and thistles," I answered. "Something weird happened when I started mowing it. I ran into a big stone—"

"That was stupid," Carl said. "You could have busted the mower."

I ignored him. "It looked like a tombstone. It had words carved on it—'Here Lies the Bugman. Woe to

14

Anyone Who Wakes Him.' And I cracked it right down the middle."

"So?" Carl said, trying to sound bored.

"Mrs. Lowy—the lady who hired me—said this guy called the Bugman lived in the house next door to her more than fifty years ago," I explained. "He studied bugs—and some people thought he was turning into one."

"And you cracked open his tombstone?" Carl asked. "Aren't you scared? The tombstone said 'Woe to anyone who wakes him.' That means you."

Carl sounded happy. "Woe! Woe! Woe! Woe!" he chanted.

Why do I bother talking to him? "Mrs. Lowy thinks some kids put the tombstone there as a joke," I said.

"And you believed her?" Carl asked. "Adults always tell kids stuff like that. She probably didn't want you to get scared."

"I wasn't scared," I said quickly. "It's just an old story." No way was I admitting the truth to Carl.

"You should be scared," Carl warned. "I've heard of the Bugman. My uncle Rich told me about him. He could control insects. He could make them do anything he wanted. Sting people. Or spy on them and report back. Or—"

"Oh, right," I snapped. I studied Carl's face. He could be making the whole thing up to torture me.

15

Or he could be telling the truth.

"Really," Carl insisted. "I heard about some kids who cut across his lawn once—and a whole swarm of wasps went after them. They got about a million stings each. And cracking his tombstone is a lot worse than walking on his lawn."

"Even if that story is true—and it isn't—the Bugman is dead now," I told him. "He's been dead for a long time."

"Yeah, you're right," Carl said. "I guess he can't do anything to you."

"I'm going in to get something to drink," I announced. I stood up. Expecting Carl to tag along—as usual.

But he didn't move. He stared up at me. His mouth hanging open. His gray eyes bulging. Not a pretty sight.

"What?" I asked.

"Freeze," he whispered. "It's starting."

Carl sounded scared. I felt my stomach twist. *"What?"*

Carl slowly pushed himself to his feet. "There is a giant wasp crawling on your shoulder. It has to be one of *his*. The Bugman is after you."

3

"**D**on't move," Carl said in a low voice, creeping closer.

"Just get it off," I whispered. I didn't know how much longer I could stand still.

"It's crawling around your back now," he whispered. "Hold it, hold it. Don't move. There!"

Whap! Carl smacked his hand down on my back—hard!

"Ha, ha! You really fell for that one!" Carl cried. He cracked up. "Get it off! Get it off!" he squeaked in that high little voice that is supposed to sound like mine.

I hate Carl. I really, really hate him.

"You jerk!" I shouted. I gave him a hard punch on the shoulder. Then I stalked into the house and slammed the door behind me.

Carl made up that whole stupid story, I reminded myself when I rode up to Mrs. Lowy's house two days later. And that tombstone is a fake. Just a dumb joke.

I parked my bike in the side yard and hurried into the garage to get gardening tools. Mrs. Lowy wasn't home—but I found the tools right where she said I would. Good.

I'll start with that bed of red and white flowers near the big tree in the front yard, I decided. I ambled over and sat down in the shade. Then I pulled on a pair of gardening gloves—I wanted to protect my hands. I had tons of blisters from all the mowing.

Weeding for money is a lot more fun than weeding for free, I thought as I worked. And in the front yard I didn't have to look at the tombstone.

My eyes wandered over to the old reddish-brown house next door. The paint was flaking off in spots, exposing a coat of dingy white paint underneath. It reminded me of somebody's skin peeling after a bad sunburn.

I turned back to the weeding. How did all the stories about the Bugman get started? I wondered.

I yanked up weed after weed. Maybe the Bugman was a scientist, I thought. That's why he spent all his time with bugs.

Or maybe his name was something like Buckman—and some little kid misunderstood it. That could have started all the weird stories. I gathered up a bunch of the weeds and stuffed them in a garbage bag.

My body felt sore all over. I pulled off my gloves and stood up. I stretched my arms over my head as high as I could, going all the way up on my toes.

Wait. I spotted someone in one of the upper-story windows next door. Someone staring down at me.

I dropped back down on my heels. Is someone in that house? It's supposed to be empty.

A drop of sweat rolled into one of my eyes. I wiped my face with the hem of my T-shirt and stared back at the house.

The curtain in the window fluttered.

I kept watching. Waiting.

No movement. Nothing.

I must have imagined it.

Back to work, I thought. I wiped my face again. Then plopped back down on the grass and pulled on one of the gardening gloves.

19

"Oww!" I shouted. Something jabbed into my finger. I yanked off the glove.

A bee! I got stung by a bee! It must have crawled inside the glove.

My finger was already red and swollen.

I jumped to my feet, shaking my hand back and forth. Trying to cool off my stinging finger.

I should run it under the hose, I thought. I dashed toward the garage—and tripped on the stone walkway.

"Are you hurt?" someone asked.

I looked up. A man loomed over me. He leaned down and peered at me through his thick, thick glasses. His eyes were huge. The biggest eyes I ever saw.

The hair on my arms stood up. The man's unblinking black eyes gave me the creeps.

"Are you all right?" he asked in a thin, high voice. "I heard you yell, then I saw you fall."

"I got a bee sting on my finger," I explained. "I was running over to the hose and I tripped."

He held out his hand. It was long and thin, and covered by a brown work glove.

I pretended I didn't notice it and stood up. The pain in my sore finger was killing me.

"Come on. I'll get you some ice," he said.

Ice would feel great on the sting. "Thanks," I answered.

He led the way across the lawn. I slowed down when I realized where he was headed. The old deserted house next door. I *did* see someone over there, I thought.

The man glanced at me curiously, so I sped up again. I shot a quick look at him. He must be hot in all those clothes. He wore a baggy long-sleeved black shirt buttoned all the way to the top, long green pants, and a floppy brown hat.

Not one speck of skin showed. Except for his face.

Weird, I thought. I stopped in the front of the porch. "Um, Mrs. Lowy told me no one lived here," I said.

"I just moved in yesterday," he answered. "I'm Mr. Cooney and I'm renting the house for the summer. I'll be right back with the ice. Sit down." He gestured to a couple of wicker chairs on the porch.

"Thanks." I could hear him humming to himself as he disappeared through the screen door. I peered after him, but I couldn't see inside the house.

A few minutes later Mr. Cooney came back out the screen door. He carried a tray with a pitcher, two glasses, and a little plastic bag full of ice.

He set the tray down and handed me the ice. "That should take the sting out," he said.

21

I pressed the ice against my finger. The skin started getting numb right away.

"Would you like some juice?" he asked. He held up a pitcher filled with green liquid.

"What kind is it?" I asked.

"Oh, it's a mixture of fresh fruits. I'm a health-food nut."

"Okay, great," I said.

He picked up a glass and filled it almost to the top. He handed it to me, then poured a glass for himself.

"Oh, my name's Janet Monroe," I told him. I set the juice on the porch rail so I could hold the ice on my finger.

"Do you live next door?" he asked, then took a long gulp of his juice.

"No. I don't live on Fear Street. The lady who lives here hired me to do yard work," I explained.

He gazed at me through his thick glasses. "This house is quite run down, as you can see," Mr. Cooney said. "The yard needs a lot of attention. Would you be interested in doing some work for me, too?"

"That would be great!" I exclaimed. I couldn't wait to tell Carl. He's going to be sorry he gave me the idea of doing yard work, I thought. Between this place and Mrs. Lowy's, I'll be making a ton of money.

Mr. Cooney smiled. "Drink your juice," he urged.

"It looks strange, but it tastes good. You can get dehydrated working in the sun all day."

I was thirsty. I set down the ice and picked up the glass. I tilted my head back, closed my eyes, and gulped down the juice.

The cold, sweet liquid felt so good.

I opened my eyes. Something brushed against my top lip, something was going into my mouth. Something prickly. I crossed my eyes, trying to see what it was.

Something dark. Something shiny.

Something alive.

4

Gross!

My stomach lurched. I spit the rest of the juice over the porch railing.

"A *beetle!*" I shrieked. "There's a beetle in my juice! And it's alive!"

Coughing and choking, I stared into the glass at the huge bug. Its wings dripped with the sticky green juice.

I dropped the glass and scrubbed my mouth with my fingers. Hard. I couldn't get the feel of that disgusting beetle off my lips.

I squeezed past Mr. Cooney. I spotted a hose near

the side of the house and raced over to it. Then I turned it on full blast.

I took a huge gulp of water. I swished it around in my mouth and spit. If I didn't get rid of that horrible feeling, I would be sick right there.

"Sorry," Mr. Cooney called from the porch. "It must have fallen in the pitcher."

I went back to the porch, picked up the glass, and reached out to drop the beetle on the ground.

"Don't!" Mr. Cooney screeched. His eyes glistened behind his glasses.

I stopped, startled.

"I'll take care of it," he continued more softly.

I handed him the glass. He carefully fished the beetle out and put it on the porch railing.

Mr. Cooney set the glass on the porch railing, too. "So, Janet, when can you start work?" he asked.

"Is tomorrow okay?" I wanted to go to the town pool after I finished Mrs. Lowy's weeding.

"Sure," he answered. "See you then."

I rode my bike straight from Mrs. Lowy's to the pool. I spread some sunscreen on my arms and legs. Then I stretched out on my big black and white beach towel. The one I got free for being the first caller to answer KLIV's music trivia question.

Some little kids splashed around in the wading pool. A few seventh graders I recognized took turns on the high dive. And a couple of guys stood around talking to the teenage girl on lifeguard duty. But I couldn't find one person I knew to hang out with.

I wish Megan would hurry up and get back from vacation, I thought. It's not that fun spending the afternoon at the pool with no one to talk to.

Oh, well. It's a lot better than weeding and mowing, I reminded myself. I closed my eyes. Enjoying the hot sun on my skin.

I like to wait until I can't stand being in the sun one more second. Then I jump right into the deep end. The cold water feels great.

Whap!

"Ow!" My stomach stung like crazy.

I didn't even have to open my eyes to know what happened. "You're dead, Carl!" I yelled. I sat up and grabbed his towel away before he could snap me with it again.

Carl laughed. "I'm sooo scared," he answered. Then he cannonballed into the pool.

Whoosh! The giant wave Carl created drenched me. "Jerk," I muttered.

Carl came up for air. Still laughing.

I leaned over and splashed water into his face until he started to choke. The lifeguard gave me a dirty look—so I stopped.

Carl hoisted himself out of the pool and plopped down next to me.

26

"I got another mowing job," I announced before he could say a word.

"Two jobs. Big deal." Carl snorted.

"Yeah, but my new job is huge. I'll be working tons—a lot more than you," I told him.

"Where is this *huge* job?" Carl demanded.

I hesitated. "Next door to Mrs. Lowy," I said.

"The *Bugman's* house?" Carl yelled. "You're working for the Bugman?"

"I'm not working for the Bugman," I protested. "I'm working for Mr. Cooney. He lives in the house where the Bugman *used* to live. The Bugman is dead—get it?"

"Big mistake," Carl said. He pointed to my leg. "Look! He sent another one of his bug friends after you."

My heart give a hard *thump*.

I felt tiny legs traveling toward my knee.

I didn't want to look. But I forced myself to glance down.

A ladybug. That's all. A little red and black ladybug crawling up my leg.

I reached down to flick it off.

"Noooooo!" someone screamed.

5

"**D**on't do that! You'll be sorry." A girl in a purple and yellow bathing suit ran toward me. "Noooo!" she screamed. "Don't do it. Leave that ladybug alone. It's bad luck."

The girl threw herself down next to me. She stuck her finger in front of the ladybug—and it crawled right on. "Poor baby," she crooned.

Carl snorted.

I didn't even glance at him. This strange girl was talking to a bug.

She looked up at me. "Sorry if I scared you by

yelling like that," the girl apologized. "But I couldn't let you hurt this little ladybug."

"It's a bug," Carl said loudly. "A stupid bug. What's your problem?"

"Every creature on earth deserves life," she told us. "That's what my whole family believes. We don't eat meat or fish or eggs. Even our cat is a vegetarian."

"Sorry," I mumbled. "I wasn't really trying to kill it. I just wanted it off me."

The girl nodded. "Most people don't ever think about bugs," she said. "If they did, they would probably treat them better."

The ladybug flew off the girl's finger. She gave it a little wave.

"What about spiders?" Carl demanded. "Or centipedes? I bet you kill them."

"I don't believe in murder," the girl answered. "When you kill anything—even a spider—you upset the balance of the universe."

Carl snorted again.

"Did you know you sound like a pig when you do that?" the girl asked.

I laughed. That's exactly what I think every time Carl gives one of his snorts.

She's cool, I decided. Weird—but cool, too. And she has to be more fun than Carl.

"I'm Janet," I told the girl. "And he's Carl."

"I'm Willow," the girl said.

"What grade are you in?" I asked. "I've never seen you at school."

"I'm going into sixth," Willow answered. "But I do home study. My family believes you can learn everything you need to know from the world around you."

Carl slid up to the edge of the pool and dangled his feet in the water. Ignoring us.

"So your parents teach you? Isn't that—" I began.

"Look!" Carl exclaimed. "There's an ant in the water. It's going to drown."

Willow scrambled next to Carl. "Where?"

"Right there!" he cried. "A big black one."

Willow leaned forward—and Carl started kicking as hard as he could. Splashing water into Willow's face.

"Carl, you idiot!" I yelled.

Willow jumped into the pool. She grabbed Carl by both feet and yanked him into the water.

Carl came up sputtering. He lunged for Willow. She twisted to the side—then dunked him again.

Definitely a cool girl, I thought.

"Say you're sorry!" Willow demanded.

"No way!" Carl choked out.

Dunk!

"Say it!" Willow ordered.

30

Carl shook his head. The stubborn expression on his face cracked me up.

Dunk!

"Okay, okay!" Carl shouted. "I'm *soooo* sorry. Are you happy now?"

"Yes," Willow told him calmly. She climbed out of the pool and sat down next to me.

"Why don't you take your new friend to the Bugman's house?" Carl urged me. "I bet they would get along great."

"Why don't you go see how long you can hold your breath under water?" I called back.

But Carl swung out of the pool and plopped himself down. He can't take a hint.

"Who's the Bugman?" Willow asked.

"He's a guy who loved bugs so much he turned into one," Carl told her. "So you better watch out. You could start growing extra legs any day." He gave Willow his best evil grin.

"Ignore him. It's just a dumb story," I protested.

The lifeguard blew her whistle. "Three o'clock," she announced. "Time for lap swimmers only. Everyone else out of the pool."

"I didn't know it was so late," Willow said. "I've got to go." She jumped up. "See you around," she called to me as she headed toward the locker room. "I come to the pool a lot."

31

Maybe this summer won't be so bad, I thought. I've got two jobs. And maybe I've found someone I can hang out with. Someone who *isn't* Carl.

I showed up at Mr. Cooney's early the next morning. I wanted to be done in time to go to the pool. I hoped Willow would be there again.

Mr. Cooney waved to me from the front porch. "I got the lawn mower out for you," he called. He pointed to a rusty mower by the porch steps.

I strolled over to it. No motor. Great, I thought. Just great.

"Do you want to borrow a long-sleeved shirt?" Mr. Cooney asked, peering down at me through those extra-thick glasses. "It isn't good for you to get too much sun, you know."

No way would Mr. Cooney ever get sunburned. He had on the same outfit as yesterday. Long pants, long-sleeved shirt buttoned all the way up, work gloves, and a hat.

Very strange guy. "No, thanks," I answered. I grabbed the mower handle. "My mom always makes me put on sunscreen."

"Okay." Mr. Cooney wandered back into the house. Humming to himself. Not a song. Just the same note over and over. *Hmm. Hmm. Hmm.*

I shook my head. He should get a Walkman, I thought.

32

I attacked the lawn. Pushing myself to mow as fast as I could.

By the time I finished, my T-shirt was glued to my back. I knew my face had to be bright red.

I checked my watch. Almost 2:10. If I hurried I could make it to the pool before 2:30.

But first I had to get paid.

I stared up at the big, old house. The curtains were drawn in every window. He must really hate the sun, I thought. I would hate to live in the dark that way.

I climbed up the porch steps. The heavy front door stood open beyond the screen. I knocked on the doorframe.

Quiet. No footsteps heading toward the door. Nothing.

I knocked again—harder.

He's got to be home, I thought. I know it. I would have noticed him leave.

I pressed my face against the screen door. But I still couldn't see anything. Too dark inside.

"Mr. Cooney?" I called. "I need to leave now!"

No answer.

I opened the door and stepped inside. The house smelled damp. Moldy.

My eyes adjusted to the dim room. A thick layer of dust covered everything—the warped wood floor, the flowered sofa, the green curtains. And there were no lamps anywhere.

This place is really creepy, I thought.

"Mr. Cooney?" I called again.

I walked down the hall.

Nothing. A door ahead of me was open a crack. I headed for it. All I wanted to do was get my money and get out of there.

I knocked on the door and it swung all the way open. I stepped inside.

There was Mr. Cooney, by a long table at the other end of the room. His back to me.

"How are you feeling today, hmm? You look well," he crooned in his high voice.

I stared around the dimly lit room. I didn't see anyone but Mr. Cooney.

"Yesss. Yesss. You are looking much better, my baby," he murmured. He turned slightly.

He raised his hand up in front of him.

Something sat there. Something black. Something hairy.

A tarantula!

Mr. Cooney brought the huge spider close to his lips.

Closer. Closer.

Then he did something that made me feel sick.

6

He kissed the spider!

How could he stand kissing a tarantula? How could he stand feeling that bristly black hair against his lips?

"I love you, my baby," Mr. Cooney cooed in his high voice. He kissed the giant spider again.

I gasped. I couldn't help it.

Mr. Cooney jerked his head toward me.

He strode across the room. The tarantula still in his hand.

I took a step backward—and bumped into the

35

doorjamb. "K-keep it away from me," I stammered. "Please."

Mr. Cooney stopped. "Oh!" he exclaimed. He returned to the table and set the tarantula down.

"I forget that everyone isn't as comfortable around spiders as I am," he apologized when he turned to face me again.

"Um, it's okay," I said in a rush. "I finished mowing the lawns. And . . . uh . . . I came to get paid."

I could hardly look at him. I'll just pretend I didn't see anything, I decided. What else could I do? Tell him what a cute spider he had? Yeah, right.

"That's fine," he answered. He didn't sound embarrassed or anything. He pulled out his wallet and handed me my pay. I put it in my pack. "Have a glass of juice before you go."

I nervously scanned the floor. Why does he have a tarantula? Does he have more than one of those spiders? I wanted out of there. Now.

"No, thanks," I blurted. "I—I have some water with me, and—"

"But your water must be warm by now," Mr. Cooney interrupted. He picked a pitcher up off the table and poured me a tall glass of the green juice.

He held the glass out to me. "Take it. It's a particularly good batch today."

I took the glass, checked it for bugs, then drank the juice in three big gulps.

I handed him the empty glass. "Thanks. I have to go. See you." I turned and rushed through the living room.

"I'll see you tomorrow," Mr. Cooney called as I slammed the screen door. Not if I see you first, I thought.

I jumped off the porch. I climbed on my bike and pedaled down the street as hard as I could.

Does he let that tarantula wander around his whole house? I wondered. I decided never to go inside again—just in case. Mr. Cooney could pay me out on the porch from now on.

He told that tarantula he loved it, I thought. That's so gross.

Suddenly I remembered what Mrs. Lowy told me about the Bugman. The Bugman loved bugs so much he started turning into one.

He *loved* bugs. And so did Mr. Cooney.

"*Janet!*" someone yelled.

I slowed down and glanced over my shoulder. Willow stood on the sidewalk.

I put on my brakes and jumped off the bike. "Didn't you hear me the first three times?" Willow complained.

"Sorry," I mumbled.

"Hey, what's wrong?" Willow asked. "You're all pale."

"It's sort of a long story," I told her. "Can you come over? I only live a couple blocks away."

"Sure," Willow answered. "I was heading over to the pool. But I can go later."

We started down the block. I walked my bike so we could talk. "You said you never heard of the Bugman, right?" I asked.

Willow nodded. Her green eyes serious.

"I hadn't, either. Until a couple days ago. . . ." I told her the whole story as we walked to my house.

Willow kicked a rock down the sidewalk. "You're giving me the creeps," she said when I got to the part about the Bugman turning into a bug. "You don't believe that story, do you?"

"No. And Mrs. Lowy said the tombstone had to be a joke. But here's the really weird part. Something really strange happened today."

We turned onto my front walk, and then I heard a familiar sound. *Shoop shoop. Shoop shoop.*

Great, I thought. All I need right now is Carl.

He zoomed past on his Rollerblades, then spun to a stop in front of us. "So what are we doing today?"

"What do you mean *we?*" I asked.

He acted as if he hadn't heard me. "You got any cookies?" He plopped down on the front porch and pulled off his skates.

"No. Go away." I rolled my eyes at Willow. She rolled her eyes back at me.

"Chips are okay then," Carl said. He stood up and walked into my house. Heading straight for the kitchen.

"Where did you find Junk Food Boy?" Willow whispered as we followed him.

"His mom and my mom are best friends," I explained. "I've known him since preschool. And I still haven't figured out how to get rid of him."

"Is that you, Janet?" my mother called from upstairs.

"Yeah!" I shouted back. "I brought a friend home. And Carl."

Willow giggled. "And Carl," she repeated.

"Make yourselves a snack," Mom answered.

Carl already had his head stuck in our refrigerator.

"So how is the Bugman?" Carl asked. He slammed the fridge door shut and opened one of the cupboards.

I didn't answer. Willow and I sat down at the kitchen table. "Come on," she urged. "Tell me what happened."

Carl grabbed a bag of Fritos and ripped it open with his teeth. He sat down across from us and shoved a handful of the corn chips in his mouth. "Something happened?" he mumbled.

"Yeah." I turned to Willow. "Today when it was time to leave, I went inside to find Mr. Cooney."

I felt the back of my neck prickle. I was getting the creeps just thinking about what happened.

"I heard him talking to someone, but no one else was in the room." I glanced back and forth between Willow and Carl. "You won't believe what he was talking to," I continued.

The prickly feeling moved up the back of my head.

"A tarantula!" Carl cried.

"How did you know?" I demanded.

My ear started to itch. I reached up to scratch it. *"Don't!"* Carl hollered.

"I'm not falling for that stupid joke again," I snapped.

"It's not a joke," Willow said quietly.

Something soft touched my cheek.

Then I caught sight of something black. Something long, and black, and hairy. Walking across my face.

7

A tarantula. A tarantula was on my face, walking onto my eyebrow.

I squeezed my eyes shut.

"Hold still," Carl said. He picked up the newspaper from the kitchen table. "I'm going to knock it off you."

"No!" Willow exclaimed. "I'll get something to put it in."

She raced over and threw open the cabinet doors—one after the other. "Don't be afraid," she called. "It won't bite you unless you scare it. And they aren't poisonous. Well, not poisonous enough to kill you."

The tarantula stepped onto my nose. Its bushy hair tickled my left nostril.

I heard Willow run back over to me. "You're okay," she said soothingly. "It's more afraid of you than you are of it."

I opened my eyes. Willow smiled in encouragement. She pressed a Tupperware container against my cheek. The she nudged the tarantula inside.

Whew!

"Put on the lid!" Carl ordered.

Willow held the lid against the container. "I can't seal it," she said. "The tarantula needs air."

I started to shake.

"It's all over," Willow said. "I'm going to make you a health shake. It will help you calm down," she added.

She picked up her purple and yellow backpack and hurried over to the kitchen counter.

I shoved my fingers through my hair. I scratched my scalp. I rubbed my face until my skin felt sore and hot. I brushed off my arms and legs.

But I kept feeling those spider legs crawling over me. Crawling everywhere. I stood up. "Carl, is there anything on my back?" I asked.

"No," he answered. His voice serious.

I studied the front of my shirt and arms and legs. Then I sat back down.

"Is it okay if I use your blender?" Willow asked.

"Yeah," I said. "There's fruit and stuff in the fridge."

"Whoa," Carl mumbled. He shook his head back and forth. "Whoa."

I stared down at the Tupperware container. I could see the tarantula moving around through the thick plastic.

Brraaap. Willow ran the blender at high speed.

A couple of minutes later she returned to the table with two thick, pale green shakes—and a Coke. She handed one of the shakes to me and the Coke to Carl. "Health shakes don't go with Fritos," she told him.

"Lucky for me," Carl answered.

"This is so weird," I muttered. "First I see a tarantula at Mr. Cooney's place. Then there's one here."

"It must have fallen into your backpack," Willow said.

"But that's not the weird part," I said. "Don't you think it's weird that a man who loves bugs would move into the Bugman's house?"

"There's only one thing that explains it," Carl said slowly.

"What?" I finally asked.

"Mr. Cooney *is* the Bugman," he answered.

"You moron," I snapped. "The Bugman is dead! That means Mr. Cooney cannot be the Bugman!"

"It's all the Fritos," Willow told me solemnly. "They're destroying his brain."

Carl shoved another handful of Fritos in his mouth. "I'm right," he mumbled. "You'll see."

The next day I fooled around as long as I could at Mrs. Lowy's. I watered the front and back lawn and did some trimming and weeding.

But I had to go over to Mr. Cooney's. He's not the Bugman, I told myself. The Bugman is dead— if there every really was a Bugman in the first place.

"Janet," Mr. Cooney called from the porch as soon as I started across his front lawn. "I got out the gardening tools for you."

I hope they're in better shape than his lawn mower, I thought. I hurried over and grabbed the tools off the porch railing.

"Have some juice before you start," Mr. Cooney said.

"No, thanks," I answered. "Mrs. Lowy just gave me a big glass of lemonade."

I turned toward the front flower bed. Mr. Cooney wasn't the Bugman. But that didn't mean I wanted to spend the morning sitting on the porch with him—especially after I saw him kiss that awful, ugly tarantula.

"I made this batch for *you*," Mr. Cooney said. I heard him climbing down the porch steps.

I sighed. Then I forced myself to smile as I turned back to him. "I'm really not thirsty," I said. "Thanks, anyway."

Mr. Cooney held a tall glass of the juice out toward me. "Drink it, Janet." His tone was sharp. And his wet black eyes gleamed behind the thick lenses of his glasses.

What is his problem? I wondered.

"Take it," he said again, his voice high and angry. "You must drink it."

No way am I drinking that stuff now, I thought. I took the glass from Mr. Cooney—and let it slip through my fingers. It shattered on the stone walkway.

"Oh, I'm so sorry!" I exclaimed. I hoped I sounded sincere.

"I'm such a klutz."

Mr. Cooney turned without a word. He marched back into the house.

He's furious at me, I thought. But I didn't care.

I bent down to pick up the pieces of broken glass. Hundreds of tiny bugs came out of nowhere. They surrounded the puddle of green juice. Hundreds. Thousands of bugs.

Sucking up the juice.

I kneeled down to get a closer look. As I watched, their bodies started to swell. To grow.

The bugs were doubling . . . no, tripling in size.

8

I stared down at the circle of insects.

What is going on here? I thought. What is in that juice? I drank that juice. *What is it doing to me?*

The screen door opened and slammed shut.

I saw Mr. Cooney rushing down the porch steps. Another big glass of the juice in his hand.

"Don't worry about spilling it," he said. "Plenty more where that came from."

I glanced down at the bugs again. They fought for the remaining juice. Their bodies still expanding.

A cricket swelled up. Growing rounder and rounder. Bigger and bigger. It sucked up more juice.

More juice—bigger and bigger.

Then *pop*. It exploded. Green goo spewed out everywhere. The other bugs swarmed around the cricket—and drank the liquid draining out of its body.

"Take the juice, Janet," Mr. Cooney whispered. "Take it."

"No!" I cried. "There's something horrible in that juice. I don't want it."

I turned and ran. Bugs crunching and squishing under my sneakers. Coating the bottoms with green slime.

"Janet!" Mr. Cooney yelled.

I didn't look back. I kept running. Running. Running.

The pool. I'll go to the pool. I'll relax. I'll think about what to do. Maybe Willow will show up. I can talk to her about this.

My side started to ache. I started to wheeze. But I didn't stop running until I reached the wire fence around the pool.

No Willow. Maybe she's in the locker room, I thought. I went over to the locker room.

I stared around. The locker room was almost empty. Just a mom trying to get her little girl to put on a pair of flip-flops.

Okay, I told myself. Calm down. You're safe now.

"What's wrong with her?" I heard the little girl ask. Her mother shushed her as they walked out.

I dropped down on one of the wooden benches and leaned forward. Trying to catch my breath.

That's when I saw it.

The scab on my knee. Shiny purple-black. About the size of a quarter—but thicker.

How did I get that? When did I hurt my knee?

I poked the scab with my finger. It felt hard. Hard and *crunchy.*

I jabbed the scab again. It cracked open . . . and oily green liquid oozed out.

Green liquid. Like Mr. Cooney's juice. My stomach lurched.

I closed my eyes and saw the cricket exploding again. Spraying green goo.

"No," I whispered. This can't have anything to do with the juice.

But it did. I knew it did.

I jumped up and rushed to the bathroom. I propped my knee up on one of the sinks and splashed it with hot water. As hot as I could stand.

Then I soaked a paper towel and covered it with the pink soap from the dispenser.

I scrubbed the scab. Scrubbed and scrubbed with the gritty soap. But it didn't come off.

The paper towel fell apart. I grabbed another one,

covered it with soap, and attacked the scab again. I had to get it off me. I had to.

This isn't working, I thought. I tossed the paper towel in the trash and started digging at the scab with my fingernails. Finally it popped off and fell into the sink.

I let my breath out with a *whoosh*. Then I ran hot water over my knee until the skin turned bright red and wrinkly.

I snapped off the water, eased my knee off the sink, and sat down on the tile floor.

I couldn't stop shivering.

Mr. Cooney's green juice did this to me, I thought. I know it. And that means . . . that means that Mr. Cooney could be the Bugman.

I slowly climbed to my feet.

I *knew* what I had to do.

I had to find out the truth about Mr. Cooney— and that green juice he kept feeding me.

I had to go back to his house.

After dark. It had to be after dark. I didn't want to get caught.

9

I stared across the dark street at Mr. Cooney's house. I'll have to get closer than this, I thought. A lot closer if I want to find out the truth about Mr. Cooney— and that disgusting green juice of his.

Okay, I decided. I'll count to three. Then I'll run over to the big pine tree in his front yard.

One. Two. Three.

I pounded across the street and pressed myself against the trunk of the tall tree. The bark felt rough against my cheek.

I peered around the tree trunk at the big old

51

house. No lights came on. I didn't hear footsteps or the sound of a door opening.

Safe. So far.

I wish Willow were here, I thought. Or even Carl.

But Willow never showed up at the pool. I didn't have her phone number or anything, so I couldn't tell her my plan.

And Carl was up in my room right now—playing tapes, eating cookies, and talking to himself. Mom and Dad thought I was up there with him. They would never suspect I slipped out while they sat watching TV.

Stop stalling, I ordered myself. Okay, now I'll count to three and climb the fence into the backyard.

I figured I'd have better luck in the back of the house. That's where I found Mr. Cooney kissing his tarantula.

One. Two. Three.

I dashed to the wooden fence and hauled myself to the top. Splinters dug into my palms. The fence groaned and creaked, shaking underneath me.

I jumped down into the backyard—and froze where I landed. Crouched down as low to the ground as possible.

Did he hear me?

I didn't move. My legs started to cramp. Worse than when our P.E. teacher Ms. Mason makes us do a million deep knee bends.

A dog barked, and I heard a guy yelling for it to shut up. Other than that, the neighborhood was still and quiet.

I circled around the house. Walking with my knees bent so I would be harder to see from the house. Almost there, I told myself. Almost there.

I pushed through the bushes that grew below the windows and strained to see inside. Too high. I stretched up onto my tiptoes—but still couldn't quite see inside. I needed something to stand on.

I glanced around the backyard. That plastic garbage can would probably work, I decided. I hope it's empty.

I squeezed back through the bushes and hurried over to the can. Good—empty. I pulled it underneath the window and flipped it over. Then I climbed on top.

The heavy plastic buckled under my weight. But the garbage can didn't collapse. Whew!

I rose up on my knees and peered into the window. I saw a big room glowing with a dim blue light.

I leaned into the room, bracing myself on the window ledge. Good thing Mr. Cooney loves bugs so much, I thought. I don't have to worry about window screens.

Tables filled the room. And on the tables stood row after row of huge glass tanks. That's where the light is coming from, I realized. The tanks.

I needed to see more. I had to go inside.

I took a deep breath and swung one leg into the room. The garbage can flew out from under me and landed with a *thud*.

He had to hear that, I thought. Should I run? No, I needed to keep going. I pulled my other leg inside and dropped to the floor.

I lifted my head—and stared straight into a tank of cockroaches. Their shiny brown bodies glistening as they climbed over a hunk of rotting meat.

I pushed myself to my feet and glanced down into the next tank. Centipedes. Thousands of them. I could hear a soft rustling sound as they crawled over one another, their antennae waving wildly. Gross.

The next tank held a brown and white rabbit. It stared up at me, its little pink nose twitching. What are you doing in here, little bunny? I thought.

The rabbit hopped toward its food bowl. And I saw the fat gray leech clinging to its stomach.

I squeezed my eyes shut for a moment. Then I opened them and forced myself to keep moving.

I felt as if I were in a maze. The tanks of insects forming hallways and corridors.

I was surrounded by bugs. Thousands and thousands of them. My skin started to itch. I could almost feel all those little legs scurrying over me.

I have to get out of here. Now, now, now. Looking at all these bugs isn't going to help me.

I wove through the rows of tanks. Rushing faster and faster. Trying to find my way to the door. Then I turned a sharp corner. What I saw made my heart give a hard thump against my rib cage.

Mr. Cooney sat hunched over an old-fashioned desk only a few feet from me. His back was turned, and he appeared absorbed in the papers in front of him.

I inched away from him. Quietly, so quietly. I didn't want to think about what he would do if he caught me spying on him.

I took a few more small steps back.

Mr. Cooney straightened up.

Did he hear me?

Mr. Cooney reached up toward the bookshelf over the desk.

Close, I thought. I glanced over at him again—and almost screamed.

Something was wrong with Mr. Cooney. Horribly wrong!

He didn't have a hand on the end of his arm.

He had a claw. An enormous claw. Sharp and gleaming.

Like the pincer of a giant bug!

55

10

Mr. Cooney stretched open his pincer and clamped down on a book.

He doesn't have hands. He's not human. Mr. Cooney is part bug!

It's the Bugman. Mr. Cooney *is* the Bugman!

I spun around—and slammed into one of the glass tanks.

I lunged for it. But I wasn't fast enough.

The tank crashed to the floor—exploding into a million shards of glass.

Tiny white maggots flew across the room. One hit

me in the forehead. It rolled down my cheek and dropped onto the floor.

"Babies!" Mr. Cooney shrieked. Then he saw me. "What have you done to my babies?"

I turned to face him. "I . . . I'm really, really sorry, Mr. Cooney. I didn't mean to. I just bumped into the tank, and, and . . ." I stammered. "I'll work it off, I promise."

"You think you can *pay* me, and my babies will be all right?" he screeched in fury. He pointed at the floor with his horrible pincer.

I stared down at the hundreds of maggots. Blindly crawling over the sharp glass.

"You hurt them!" Mr. Cooney exploded. He glared at me through his thick glasses. "Some of them might even be dead!"

"I'm sorry," I repeated. "I'm so, so sorry."

"Sorry," Mr. Cooney snarled. "Sorry." He stalked toward me, the broken glass crunching under his feet. "My babies are dead and you're *sorry?*"

Mr. Cooney reached up and tore off his thick glasses. Ragged pieces of skin pulled away with them. His nose fell onto the floor with a moist *plop!*

I screamed. Screamed until my throat felt raw.

Mr. Cooney grabbed a strip of skin from his forehead and yanked it away. He threw it down on the floor in front of my feet.

I clenched my teeth together to keep from screaming again. A low moan escaped my lips. I shook my head back and forth, back and forth.

He tore off his right ear. Ripped away his left. Oily green goo spattered across the floor.

Mr. Cooney gave a high squeal. He peeled away his lips.

A mask! His whole face is a mask, I realized.

Now I saw the real Mr. Cooney. The real *Bugman*.

He had the head of a giant fly. No nose. A sucker for a mouth. His skin covered with rough black bristles.

And his eyes. His eyes were the worst. They bulged away from his head. Wet and shiny.

They were divided into sections—like two enormous golf balls. I could see myself reflected over and over—in each part of his black eyes.

Mr. Cooney grabbed his floppy white hat and yanked it off. A long pair of antennas uncurled. One shot out and brushed against my cheek. It felt dry and rough.

Run, my mind ordered. Run!

But I couldn't. My legs wouldn't move. They felt rooted to the floor.

I couldn't look away from Mr. Cooney.

I heard a horrible moist sucking sound. I gazed around wildly. What is that?

I realized the sound came from Mr. Cooney's mouth.

He leaned closer toward me, his eyes glistening with anger.

And spat a stream of bright green liquid at me.

12

The green spit splattered across my bare arm. Bubbling and foaming until it soaked into my skin.

My skin turned dead white. And cold. Cold clear through to the bone. So cold it burned.

I heard Mr. Cooney making that sucking sound again. He's getting ready to spit! I realized.

I jumped back. I grabbed the closest tank and heaved it off the table. It shattered on the floor between me and Mr. Cooney. Pieces of glass flew across the room.

Hundreds of red ants poured out of the tank. The biggest ants I had ever seen.

Mr. Cooney shrieked in agony. He lunged toward me—his pincer clicking open and shut.

I dived under the nearest table—grinding the ants under my hands and knees. Their bites felt like hot needles jabbing into my skin, but I didn't stop. I couldn't stop.

I crawled out the other side and shoved the table over. Two more tanks crashed to the floor. I heard a furious buzzing, but I didn't look back to find out which insects I had released.

I dashed for the window. Stumbling as I followed the twists and turns of the maze of tanks.

I heard Mr. Cooney crooning to his *babies*. Then I heard him coming after me. His pincer snapping open and shut. *Click, click, click.*

I leaped for the windowsill and hauled myself on top. I wriggled through the opening on my stomach. I could see the backyard. See the grass and the trees and the lawn. Almost there. Almost there, I thought.

I pushed off with both hands—and something grabbed my foot. Squeezing it tighter and tighter. I twisted around and stared over my shoulder.

I saw Mr. Cooney's pincer locked around my ankle. "You're not going anywhere!" he shouted.

I kicked frantically. Tried to squirm away. Then I reached out of the window as far as I could and grabbed one of the bushes with both hands.

I pulled myself toward the bush. Fighting to hold on to the tiny branches.

Mr. Cooney yanked on my foot—hard. I almost lost my grip. He yanked again.

My shoe popped off in his pincer, and I fell face first into the bush.

I jumped up and ran. Raced around the house, over the fence, across the front lawn.

Is he following me? I didn't stop to check.

Tiny stones dug through my sock and into my foot. But I couldn't stop. Didn't stop until I reached my front door.

I pulled open the door and stumbled into the hallway. "Mom," I croaked. My throat too dry to yell. "Mom!" I tried again.

The room whirled around me. I felt dizzy, so dizzy. I couldn't stand up. I collapsed on the hard floor of the front hall.

My eyes drifted shut. I knew I should try to yell for help. But I felt too weak, too woozy.

I felt a cold hand on my forehead.

"Janet!" a voice called. It sounded so far away. "Janet, what's wrong?"

I forced my eyes halfway open. Mom!

"Is she okay?" someone else asked. I thought it was Carl.

"Mom," I mumbled. "Bugman's after me. He spit on me. I spilled his maggots . . . I mean his babies.

He likes to call them his babies. Didn't mean to, Mom."

My eyes fluttered shut again. I couldn't hold them open a moment longer.

"You're burning up," I heard Mom say. She sounded even farther away now. "You have a fever. But you're okay. . . . You're going to be okay. . . ."

I shook my head back and forth. I felt the floor rock beneath me. "No, no, no," I protested. "Don't understand. Don't understand, Mom. He pulled his *face* off. And he spit at me. And he's going to come after me."

"Herb!" Mom called in her teeny, tiny voice. Why did her voice sound so funny? "Herb, there's something wrong with Janet!"

I heard Dad running up. He touched my head with his big hand. "You're right. She's on fire."

"You go on home, Carl," Mom said. "I'll call your mother later."

"Dad," I begged. "You have to help me get away. The Bugman is coming. And he's so mad at me. I broke open his tombstone and then I hurt his babies. But I didn't mean to. I didn't mean to."

"It's like the time when she was six, remember?" Mom asked. I could hardly hear her. "She had a high fever and thought a man-eating plant was growing in her stomach."

"Let's get her to bed." I felt Dad scoop me up in his arms.

"I'm going to call the doctor," Mom answered.

All the colors in the room ran together, swirling around me. Swirling in front of my eyes. I couldn't see Mom and Dad anymore. But I knew Dad was carrying me up the stairs.

He put me down on the bed and pulled off my other shoe. The colors in front of my eyes faded. My head cleared a little.

That's when I saw it. On my arm. Right where the Bugman's spit landed.

A shiny purple-black scab about as big as my fist.

"No. No, no, no," I moaned.

I reached down and rubbed my fingers over the spot. It felt thick and hard. And *crunchy*.

Like the shell of a giant beetle.

13

"**D**ad, I'm turning into a bug. You've got to help me. Please." I struggled to sit up, but my dad pressed me back onto the bed.

"Shhh. Shhh," Dad coaxed. "You're safe, Janet. Nothing bad is going to happen to you. I'm right here."

I clawed at the big scab. I had to pull it off.

Dad caught both my hands in one of his. "Don't, Janet."

He doesn't understand, I thought. I have to make him understand.

I concentrated as hard as I could. Start at the

65

beginning, I thought. "Listen, please," I begged him. "I was mowing. *Mowing*. And I hit a tombstone—the Bugman's tombstone. And he's mad. He's so mad at me, Dad."

"No, no, Janet," Dad crooned. "He's not mad. Who could be mad at you?"

Mom rushed in and sat down on the bed next to me. I stared up at her. "Mom, I'm a bug. Dad doesn't understand. I'm a *bug*."

"She's delirious," Dad said softly.

Mom slipped the thermometer under my tongue. "Don't talk now, Janet. We have to see how high your temperature is."

I opened my mouth to try and explain again. But my mom grabbed my chin lightly between her fingers. "You can't talk now. Keep still—only for a minute, okay?"

They're never going to believe me, I thought. Never.

"I called Dr. Walker," my mom told my dad. "She's out of town. I told her service it was an emergency, so the doctor who is covering for her is coming right over. He's supposed to be very good, too."

Doctor, I thought. Maybe a doctor could help me.

Mom pulled the thermometer out of my mouth. "A hundred and four," she said.

I lay still, focusing on what I needed to tell the doctor.

"Do you want some ice water, honey?" Mom asked.

I shook my head. I need to rest now, I thought. Rest so I can tell the doctor what the Bugman did to me. Maybe he can do tests on that green goo. That green goo in the scab.

I raised my arm and stared at the purple-black scab. "It's bigger," I whispered. "It's *growing.*"

"What, baby?" Mom asked.

I shook my head. "Nothing," I mumbled. I knew she wouldn't believe me. I lowered my arm back to my side.

I shivered. How long would it take for the scab to get so big it covered my whole arm? My whole *body?*

The doctor has to help me, I thought.

Mom pulled my extra comforter out of the closet and spread it over me. "You're shaking," she said.

The doorbell rang. "That should be the doctor," Mom told me.

"He'll fix you right up," Dad promised as we waited.

My door opened and Mom stepped back in. "Honey, this is Dr. Brock. He's not your usual doctor—but he's filling in for Dr. Walker until Dr. Walker is back from vacation."

I hope he'll listen to me, I thought. If he doesn't . . .

Mom led the doctor into the room.

I stared up at him. Baggy long-sleeved shirt. Long green pants.

He leaned toward me. Peering at me through thick, thick glasses. His black eyes glittering.

"Noooo!" I yelled. "Get him away from me. He's the Bugman!"

14

The Bugman! He followed me.

"It's the Bugman!" I shouted. "I have to get out of here!"

I threw off the comforter and scrambled out of bed. But before I got halfway to the door, Dad grabbed my by the shoulders.

Dad wouldn't let go. He turned me around to face the Bugman. I opened my mouth to scream again.

Wait. Wait. It isn't the Bugman.

The doctor wore the same thick glasses. But the doctor had curly blond hair. He smiled at me gently.

"Janet, this is Dr. Brock, Dr. Brock," my mother repeated over and over.

I nodded. "I'm sorry," I mumbled. I felt like such an idiot. I returned to the bed and sat down.

"It's okay," Dr. Brock answered. "Most people with high fevers have some strange thoughts."

Oh, no! He'll never believe me now. He'll never believe that the Bugman has done something horrible to me!

Dr. Brock did all the usual stuff. Made me cough while he listened with the stethoscope. Used a little light to check my eyes. Looked in my ears and throat.

"Nothing serious," he told my parents. "I'll give you a prescription for some antibiotics. Janet will be fine in no time."

"What about this scab?" I blurted out. I held up my arm.

Dr. Brock turned to me. He ran his fingers over the huge purple-black scab.

I have to at least try and get him to help me, I thought. "This happened when the Bugman spit at me. The spit was bright green. It landed right there." I pointed to the scab.

"I'll get you an ointment for that," Dr. Brock told me. He glanced at my parents. "If it doesn't start clearing up in a few days, let me know."

70

"Please listen. Mom, Dad, make him listen," I begged. "Break open the scab. There is this green stuff in it. *Green.* Like the juice the Bugman gave me to drink."

I scratched the scab with both hands, trying to show them the oily green mucus. "You can do tests on it!" I cried.

My parents each grabbed one hand. "Calm down, sweetie. Calm down," Mom pleaded.

"This medicine should take the fever down," Dr. Brock said. "It may make her very sleepy, but right now she needs a lot of rest."

"No!" I protested. No, I can't sleep. I have to do something. The scab was growing. The Bugman was after me. If I went to sleep now . . .

Dr. Brock handed me two tiny pills. Mom gave me the glass of ice water from my bedside table.

I tried to swallow the water without swallowing the pills—but they started to dissolve in my mouth. They tasted so bitter I swallowed them before I could stop myself.

"Bye, Janet," Dr. Brock said. "Call me if the fever doesn't break," he added to my mom.

"We'll let you sleep now," my dad said. "We'll be right downstairs if you need us."

Okay, I thought as my parents and Dr. Brock left the room. I'll wait for a while, then I'll sneak out.

I yawned. I felt so tired. So sleepy.

I stretched out on the bed. I'll close my eyes, I thought. Just for a minute. Just for a minute.

When I opened my eyes, I couldn't see anything. Blackness surrounded me.

"Mom," I called. My mouth felt dry and gritty. "Mom?" I tried again. No answer.

The bed felt so hard. And cold.

I squinted, trying to see through the darkness. Tiny dots of light came into focus. Hundreds of dots of light.

Stars, I realized. Those are stars!

I'm outside!

How did I get out here? Did I sleepwalk?

I tried to sit up—but I couldn't. I couldn't move.

What is going on? I thought. What's happening to me now?

I fought to lift my head, the muscles in my neck straining. Then I stared down at my body.

A low moan escaped from my throat. My body . . . I was buried in mud up to my neck.

How did I get out here?

Who did this to me?

"Mom!" I yelled. But my throat was too dry to make much sound. She would never hear me from all the way down here.

I struggled to sit up again. But the mud was packed tightly around me.

No, not just mud, I realized. A mix of mud and leaves and twigs that formed a shell around me.

No! Not a shell.

A *cocoon!*

15

I pulled my hands out of the muddy cocoon and started to pull the leaves and twigs off me. As I did, parts of a dream came back to me. I saw myself climbing out of bed—walking to this tree and working to build this cocoon. But it wasn't a dream. It was real. I made this cocoon because I'm turning into a bug.

The Bugman is turning me into a huge bug. I'll end up exactly like him.

"Noooo," I wailed. "No, I don't want to be a bug!" I had to stop him. Somehow I had to stop him.

I struggled to kick my feet and break through the shell. I could only get my toes to move a few inches.

I dug harder with my hands, tearing at the mud on my legs.

Hurry, hurry, hurry, I ordered myself. I didn't know how much time I had. How long would the transformation take? How long would I still be human?

I wriggled and kicked until my legs broke free.

Then I scrambled up. I was covered with leaves and twigs and grass and mud. I brushed off as much as I could. I touched my arms and legs searching for more of those horrible scabs. But the mud was too thick.

I tiptoed to the back door and opened it as quietly as I could. I didn't want Mom or Dad to see me like this. They wouldn't believe me. They would get the doctor back here in a second.

I didn't turn on the lights. I crept through the kitchen and down the stairs to the basement. I washed up at the big sink.

The scab on my arm was a little bigger. But I didn't see any other changes. At least not yet.

I put on clean clothes from the laundry basket and rolled the muddy ones into a little ball. I stuffed them behind the dryer. I'd figure out what to do with them later.

75

I had no time now. All that mattered was getting to the Bugman.

I reached the kitchen door. It swung open before I could grab the doorknob.

"Janet!" my mom exclaimed. "What are you doing down there? I went into your room to check on you and you were gone."

Oh, no! Now what am I going to do? I didn't have one second to waste.

"Um, I guess I was sleepwalking," I told her. "I'll just go back up to bed." I tried to rush past her.

"That happened when you were nine and had a fever," Mom answered. She followed right behind me. "I'll sit with you until you fall asleep."

I'm doomed. Doomed, I thought. There is no way out of this.

I had no choice. I followed Mom upstairs.

Tap. Tap. Tap.

Mom poked her head in the door. "You had a good sleep," she said. She hurried over and pressed her hand on my forehead. "And your fever is down."

"I feel fine," I answered. I swung my legs off the bed. I had to convince Mom to let me outside.

"Not so fast," she said. "You're going to spend the day in bed. But your friend Willow is downstairs if you feel well enough to see her."

"Willow? Yes! I want to see her. Please," I said in a rush.

"For a short visit," Mom answered. "You're not over this virus yet." She headed downstairs. A few minutes later Willow peeked into my room.

"Come inside and close the door," I ordered her. "I have something really important to tell you."

Willow rushed over and sat down on my bed. "Your mom said you were really sick," she said.

"The Bugman is doing something horrible to me," I began. "I think he's turning me into a bug. You've got to help me."

Willow tried to smile. But she looked worried.

"Oh—my mother must have told you I would say that," I said. "She thinks my fever made me delirious or something. But it didn't. And anyway I feel fine now."

I took a big breath and hurried on. "I went to the Bugman's house yesterday—"

"What?" Willow interrupted.

"I had to," I answered. "I had to try and find a way to stop him."

"Wait, wait. Slow down," Willow protested. "What happened after I saw you that day with the tarantula?"

"I went to Mr. Cooney's the next day. He wanted me to drink more of this green juice he makes—he's been giving it to me every day since I met him. I

77

wouldn't. I dropped the glass on the ground. All these bugs started drinking it—and getting bigger and bigger."

"But—" Willow began.

"Let me finish," I said. I could tell Willow was ready to interrupt again. I talked faster and faster so she wouldn't have a chance. I needed to tell her everything before my mom came back upstairs.

"Last night he caught me spying on him—and he ripped his face right off," I continued. "His human face was a mask. He really has the head of a giant fly or something."

"Whoa," Willow whispered. She hesitated. "Janet, don't get mad, okay? Couldn't your mom be right? Couldn't you have imagined the whole thing?"

"No way!"

Willow held up her hand. "Listen. When you're sick you can have some really weird dreams, even visions. I remember when I—"

"It wasn't a dream!" I insisted. *"Or* a vision. It wasn't.

"You've got to help me figure out a way to get back over to the Bugman's house. My mom will hardly let me out of her sight. But if I don't figure out what he's doing to me—I won't be able to stop him."

"Okay, okay," Willow said softly. "I believe you."

Willow thought for a minute. "I'll go for you," she

78

said. "It's the only way. We'd never be able to sneak you out past your mom."

"No. No, you can't go over there alone. It's too dangerous," I told her.

"I'll be careful. I'll look for evidence that he can turn people into bugs. And maybe I can get a sample of that juice," Willow said.

"I don't know," I said. "It's too scary. He really is a monster."

"Don't worry," Willow whispered. "I'll be careful. I'll go to his house right now. Don't worry. We'll find a way to stop the Bugman together."

"Thank you," I said. "Thank you so, so much. You're the best, Willow."

"I'll come back here as soon as I'm done," Willow promised. She jumped up and rushed out the door without looking back.

I climbed out of bed and stared down at the front yard. I watched Willow run out of the door and head toward Fear Street.

I rubbed my fingers over the scab on my arm. Bigger. Definitely bigger.

I watched Willow turn down Fear Street. Toward the Bugman's house.

Was she already too late?

16

I climbed back in bed and pulled my comforter up to my chin. Mom brought up some magazines, but I couldn't concentrate on reading. All I could think about was Willow.

I tried to picture every step she made—so I would know when to expect her back.

Okay. She left my room, walked down the stairs, said bye to my mom. Then put on her purple and yellow backpack, went out the front door, and ran down the street.

I could imagine everything Willow did—until she got to the Bugman's house. Then I couldn't come up with anything. I didn't know what would happen there.

And I couldn't do anything to help Willow. That was the worst.

I checked the clock. 11:14. Not even an hour since Willow left.

I asked Mom to bring the little TV from the kitchen upstairs. But even the wacko people on the talk shows couldn't hold my attention.

I checked the clock again. 1:00.

She should be back by now, I thought. I picked at the ragged skin around my thumbnail. She really should be back by now.

Maybe she had to wait for the Bugman to leave the room where his desk is. That could take a while.

Mom brought me up some lunch. I wasn't very hungry, but I ate some anyway. Then I tried to take a nap. But I couldn't fall asleep.

I rolled over onto my side and stared at my scab. Was it really bigger? Were there more of them? I couldn't tell anymore.

I looked at my alarm clock. Watching the seconds and minutes change. Waiting for Willow.

2:00. 3:00. 4:00. 5:00. No Willow.

Maybe I should call Carl and ask him to look for her. But the phone was downstairs. Mom might hear me.

Mom would think I was delirious again. I couldn't

risk her giving me another sleeping pill. I had to stay awake. I had to wait for Willow.

Dad came up to visit. I didn't feel like talking.

6:00. 7:00. 8:00. No Willow. And it would be dark soon.

I crawled out of bed and stared out the window. The street stood empty. What am I going to do if she doesn't come back?

9:00. 10:00. No Willow.

It was too dark to see anything out the window. I paced around my room. I felt too nervous to stay still.

Mom and Dad came in to say good night.

11:00. No Willow.

The Bugman has Willow!

Willow was trying to help me—and the Bugman got her. I knew it.

I'm sneaking out, I decided. I have to. I have to save Willow.

I pulled on jeans, sneakers, and a long-sleeved black T-shirt and started for my bedroom door. No. I couldn't risk going out the front way. I would have to walk right past Mom and Dad's bedroom—and one of them would hear me.

I opened my window and crawled out onto the garage roof. I slowly inched my way down to the edge and looked over. I grabbed the gutter and slid to the ground, holding on to the drainpipe.

I made it!

I took off for Fear Street. Please let me be in time, I thought. Please.

The Bugman's house stood dark and silent. I climbed over the back fence.

The garbage can. Where is it? I thought. I looked around. Then I saw something that made me gasp.

A piece of purple and yellow cloth rested on top of the Bugman's tombstone. It had to be Willow's. She always wore those colors.

I looked at the house. Still dark. I hurried over to the tombstone.

I grabbed the yellow and purple material. It's Willow's backpack, I realized.

Suddenly the ground rumbled and shook.

I fell onto the Bugman's tombstone.

What's happening? I thought. An earthquake?

Craaack!

The tombstone broke in half. The earth underneath it began to crumble.

A pit opened up. The two big pieces of granite started to slide into the pit.

I threw myself off the stone. Digging my fingers into the grass and weeds. Holding on, desperately clutching at the ground. Tearing at the dirt. Grabbing anything to keep from falling into the pit.

The earth bucked and shook. But I hung on—my legs dangling over the gaping pit.

83

Then the ground stopped shaking.

Still. Quiet. I crawled away from the pit—scraping my knees on stones and twigs.

Something sharp clamped around my ankle. It tore through the leg of my jeans.

I twisted around. "Noooo!" I shrieked.

The Bugman. He jerked on my ankle, pulling me down.

Down into his grave!

17

"**S**top!" I screamed. "Let me go!"

The Bugman tightened his grip on my foot and yanked it hard.

I couldn't hold on. I slid into the grave. Down. Down. Down.

The earth rumbled, closing in around me. I couldn't see. My mouth and nose filled with dirt.

I couldn't breathe. My lungs ached and burned.

Then I was falling. Falling through the air.

Thunk!

I landed at the bottom of the grave. I sat up, coughing and choking.

I heard a sound behind me. I jumped up and turned around fast. The Bugman stood there watching me.

A whimper escaped from my throat. For the first time I saw the Bugman's true form. I couldn't stop staring at him.

His back . . . his back was covered by a shiny purple-black shell. The same color as the scab on my arm!

His legs were as skinny as broom handles.

And he had four arms. Two arms the regular human size and shape. And two shorter, thinner arms growing out of the center of his chest.

Each arm ended in a sharp pincer. The Bugman clicked them open and shut as he studied me with his enormous eyes. *Click! Click! Click! Click!*

"Come with me," the Bugman ordered in his high voice. He grabbed my wrist in his pincer. Then he pulled me through a narrow dirt tunnel.

We entered a large chamber—bigger than the first—filled with a strange yellow glow.

Where is that light coming from? I knew we were still underground.

Lightning bugs! Lightning bugs are giving the light, I realized. They clung to the sides of the hollowed-out room. Thousands of them, blinking on and off in different rhythms.

"Hello, hello, my dears," the Bugman crooned. He

released my wrist and scuttled over to the wall. "My sweet darlings," he called to the lightning bugs.

"I told everyone about you!" I shouted. "They will come looking for me—so you better let me out of here right now!"

The Bugman gave a high, shrill shriek. He spun toward me. I felt his hot breath hit my face. It smelled like rotting lettuce.

Then I heard a sucking, slurping sound. He's going to spit on me again! I covered my face with my arms and backed away from him.

"Janet!"

I recognized the voice at once!

"Willow? Where are you?" I stared around the large room.

"I'm here. On the floor."

Then I saw her. Wrapped in a cocoon from her neck to her feet.

I dashed over to her and kneeled down next to her. "The Bugman got you, too! Are you okay?"

She looked past me and smiled. "See? I *told* you she would come, Father!"

18

Father?

"No. No, Willow!" I cried. "The Bugman can't be your father. He must have given you something to make you believe that."

I grabbed the top of Willow's cocoon. "I'm tearing you out of there!" I yelled.

"Janet, don't!" Willow shouted. "You'll hurt me!"

The Bugman grabbed me by the back of my shirt and threw me against the wall. Then he came toward me. *Click! Click! Click! Click!*

"No, Father!" Willow exclaimed. "Don't hurt her! She's my friend. I want her for my friend."

The Bugman stared at me with his enormous black eyes. "I want you to be my Willow's friend, Janet. I won't hurt you—as long as you don't hurt Willow or the babies."

He really is her father, I realized. Willow tricked me. She planned to get me here all along!

"Why did you do this to me?" I yelled at Willow.

The Bugman began to hum. A high, whining sound.

How will I ever get out of here? What am I going to do? Mom and Dad don't know where I went. Maybe there's a way.

"I wanted you to be my friend," Willow said.

She sounded hurt. I couldn't believe it.

"You've got to listen to me. Please," Willow begged.

The Bugman pointed at her with one sharp pincer. Silently ordering me over to her.

I'll go along with them for a while, I decided. Until I can figure out what to do. I shuffled back over to Willow and sat down next to her cocoon.

"Okay. I'm listening. What?" I asked.

"I needed a friend. And I picked you," Willow answered. I noticed her green eyes glistening with tears.

"We *are* friends," I protested. I didn't want to

89

make Willow—or her father—upset again. Not until I found a way out of there.

"You don't understand," she said. "You can't really be my friend. Not the way you are. No one can."

I took a quick peek at the Bugman. He stood only a few feet behind me.

"Why not?" I asked.

"Because I'm only human part of the time. For two years I'm a girl. Then I go into a cocoon and spend two years as—"

"As a *bug?*" I interrupted. My stomach turned over.

"Yes. And it's so lonely. I make new friends. And then I lose them." Willow smiled up at me. "But now Father figured out a way to change you, too. Now we can be friends forever. Isn't that great?"

Great? She's nuts, I thought.

"I don't want to be a bug, Willow," I explained.

"Oh, you'll love it! You get to live in two worlds this way," Willow said. "You really feel part of the great circle of life. It's awesome!"

"But what about my family?" I asked. "I'll miss them."

"Father and I will be your family," Willow reassured me.

What could I say now? "But . . . but your father hates me. I destroyed his tombstone. I woke him from the dead."

Hmmm. Hmmm. Hmmm. The Bugman had started his humming again. But it sounded different. Lower. Not so piercing.

I glanced back at him. He rocked back and forth on his thin, thin legs, rubbing his pincers together. *Hmmm. Hmmm. Hmmm.*

The Bugman is laughing! I realized.

"What's so funny?" I asked.

"I was never dead," he answered in his high voice. "I was hibernating. A trick I learned from the seven-year locusts."

"But what about the tombstone?" I asked.

"Some boys put it there," the Bugman told me. "They became frightened of me once I began experimenting on myself. They didn't understand the thrill of transformation—of becoming half bug and half human."

The Bugman shook his head. "A group of them took me from my home and buried me in the yard," he continued. He began to click his pincers open and shut. "They thought I was dead. They put the tombstone on top of me."

He made his laughing-humming sound again. "But I wasn't dead. I was hibernating."

I swallowed hard. The Bugman could never be destroyed! I was trapped.

"See, Janet?" Willow said. "We'll be giving you a great new life. You'll live hundreds more years than most people."

"Thank you. I appreciate it, really," I told the Bugman. Then I turned my gaze to Willow. "But please choose someone else. I know it doesn't make sense to you, but I want to stay human."

"It's too late for that," the Bugman said. "The process has already begun."

My heart pounded so loud I could hardly hear him. "What?" I cried.

The Bugman scurried over to the dirt wall behind Willow. "Excuse me, babies," he said. He gently shooed some of the fireflies away.

Now I could see a small hole dug into the wall. A pitcher sat inside it. The same pitcher the Bugman used to serve the green juice.

Then I understood. "I was right!" I yelled. I jumped to my feet. "That juice you kept giving me — and the health shake Willow made — it's already started turning me into a bug."

"Yes," the Bugman answered. He picked up the pitcher and started toward me. "Now, have some more."

"No!" I shouted.

"Please, Janet. Be reasonable," the Bugman said.

"Never! Let me out of here!"

"Very well," the Bugman said firmly. "Babies! Do your work!"

19

Hundreds of bugs swarmed through the earth and came toward me. Beetles. Ants. Centipedes.

Something soft brushed against my face. Soft and sticky. I looked up. "No," I whispered.

A fat gray spider hung on a shiny thread in front of my nose. Another spider slithered down. Faster and faster, they dropped their threads around me.

I slashed my hand across the threads, and the spiders fell to the ground. More spiders slid down to take their place.

My ankles started to itch and burn. I stared down.

The cuffs of my jeans bulged as the army of bugs shoved their way inside.

I shook one leg, then the other. Bugs tumbled back onto the ground. But more kept coming.

Then I heard buzzing—getting louder and louder. I squeezed my eyes shut. I didn't want to see the wasps and bees arrive.

"Willow!" I screamed. "Help me! Please!"

Bugs flew into my mouth. I choked, coughing and spitting.

"It will be okay, Janet," Willow called. "Don't fight it. Let them build the cocoon. It's the final stage."

Cocoon? They're building a cocoon?

I opened my eyes. Every inch of my body was covered with bugs.

I tried to knock them off. But I couldn't. My arms were pinned to my sides.

The spiders are spinning webs around me, I realized. That's why I can't move.

A row of ants climbed onto my face. Each carried tiny twigs and pieces of leaves. They stuck to my skin.

The bees and wasps dive-bombed me. Dropping more leaves and bits of wax and honey.

Then all the insects turned and swarmed away from me. Burrowing into the soil. Climbing back into the ceiling. Flying out the tunnel.

"It's almost over," Willow called.

Almost?

The earth moved again. And rows and rows of thick yellow slugs burst through. They slithered toward me, and then crept up my body.

Their cold slime trails sealed the cocoon even more tightly.

I couldn't move at all.

The Bugman's babies had finished their work. They slid off me and disappeared.

"Time to sleep now," the Bugman announced in a singsong voice. He scurried over to Willow with the pitcher of green juice. He bent down and poured some into her mouth.

"See you when we wake up, Janet!" Willow cried. "Just think of this as a slumber party—with our cocoons as sleeping bags."

"Willow, no. Tell your father you changed your mind," I pleaded.

But she didn't answer.

The Bugman kissed Willow on the forehead. "Good night, Princess," he said.

"Good night, Father," she said. The Bugman placed a loose hood over her head. It looked as if it were made of spiderwebs.

Then the Bugman turned to me.

"No," I begged. "Please don't do this. Please. I

want to go home to my family. I want to stay human."

The Bugman shook his head. "It will all be over soon," he said. He pressed the pitcher of juice against my lips.

20

I twisted my head back and forth violently. I couldn't drink that juice.

The Bugman uttered a high, angry whine. He trapped my head between two of his pincers and forced the spout of the pitcher between my lips.

"Drink!" he ordered.

I clenched my teeth. Clenched them until my jaws ached.

Then the Bugman clamped my nose closed with one pincer. I couldn't breathe.

My chest started to burn. But I didn't open my

mouth. My heart thudded harder and harder. But I kept my teeth locked together.

Air, I thought. I need air.

Tiny red dots burst in front of my eyes.

I had to have air.

I opened my mouth and sucked in a big breath.

I tried to slam my teeth shut again. Too slow. The Bugman tilted back my head and poured the green juice into my mouth.

No! I won't drink it, I thought.

I spit it out—aiming for the Bugman's black eyes.

He squealed in pain. Got him!

The Bugman dropped the pitcher onto the ground and stumbled away from me. He scrubbed at his eyes with all four pincers.

"You are not worthy of being my daughter's friend!" the Bugman screamed. His antennae whipped back and forth. Green drool dripped from his mouth. He began snapping all four pincers open and closed.

I wiggled and squirmed, trying to break free of the cocoon. But the webbing was too tight. My arms stayed glued to my sides. And my feet were locked together.

"I was going to give you a beautiful life—but you're not worthy!" the Bugman shrieked. "Now you must be *exterminated!*"

21

The Bugman charged at me.

I threw my weight forward—and slammed into him. We both fell.

I rolled over and over, still trapped in my tight cocoon. Then I thudded to a stop against the crumbly dirt wall.

The Bugman gave a shrill squeal.

He's coming after me, I thought. And I can't even stand up.

I twisted my neck around. Where is he?

Then I saw him. He lay flat on his big purple-black shell. All four arms and his skinny legs waved wildly in the air.

He can't stand up! I knocked him over. He landed on his back—and he can't flip himself back over.

"Babies!" the Bugman cried. "Babies, help me. Help me."

All the bugs swarmed back up from the floor and walls and ceiling. Thousands of them. They crawled over the Bugman.

What if they are strong enough to help him up? I had to get out of the cocoon. Fast.

I rolled back and forth, struggling to break free of the webbing. But the cocoon didn't feel any looser.

I grabbed hold of the webbing under my chin the only way I could. With my teeth.

I gave it a yank—and a piece ripped off. I spit it out and bit into another section, the leaves and twigs crunching in my mouth. Gross!

I tore away as much of the webbing as I could reach. The cocoon felt looser now, and I could move one arm a little.

I glanced over at the Bugman. I couldn't see him at all. The insects covered him completely.

Hurry, I ordered myself. If his babies flip him right side up, you're dead.

I worked my arm back and forth until it burst free. I tore at the cocoon until I could use my other arm, too. Faster, faster, I thought.

101

I ripped a big piece of webbing off my legs and then kicked my way out of the bottom of the cocoon. I struggled to my feet and raced down the narrow tunnel.

I could still hear the Bugman screaming. Then I heard another voice. Willow's.

"Janet," Willow called. "Don't go! Don't you want to be my friend?"

I didn't answer. There is nothing I can do for her, I told myself. The tunnel split in two directions. One seemed to run uphill. I followed it, the dirt making me choke and cough.

The tunnel hit a dead end. I dug frantically, bringing down clumps of dirt on my head. Then I felt a cool breeze on my face—and saw the stars shining above me.

As I hauled myself through the hole I heard Willow's voice echo through the tunnel behind me. "Janet. Don't go. Stay. Don't you want to be my friend?"

Epilogue

*W*hap!

"Oww!" My back stung like crazy. I sat up and grabbed the beach towel out of Carl Beemer's hands. "You jerk!" I yelled.

Carl laughed and cannonballed into the pool, sending a tidal wave onto my notebook. He came up smirking.

"Jerk," I muttered again. Megan would be back tomorrow. And Anita and Sara would be home on Friday. I couldn't wait.

Carl swam over and rested his arms on the edge of

the pool. I held up my sopping notebook. "You got water all over my story," I snapped.

"You should change it anyway," Carl answered. I noticed he didn't bother to apologize. Typical.

"I think you should make me the hero," Carl continued. "I could run into the Bugman's lair and rescue you and Willow and get my picture in the paper."

"Yeah, right," I said. "As if you would do something that brave."

I smoothed the wrinkly pages of the notebook. "I just finished the end."

"Let's hear it," Carl said.

" 'Nobody knew what happened to the Bugman or Willow after that,' " I read. " 'They disappeared— and only the Bugman's big purple-black shell was ever found.

" 'But what I cared about was that I was still *me*. Not a bug. Just a girl. A *human* girl. The End.' "

Carl snorted. He sounds like a hog when he does that. "Not bad," he admitted. "You might win that story contest in the paper. Since *I* didn't bother to write one myself."

He splashed some water in my face. "Yeah. It took a wild imagination to come up with a wacko story like that," Carl added. "What are you going to call it anyway?"

104

I thought for a minute. " 'The Bugman Lives!' " I announced.

I headed for home, my hair still wet from the pool. A beautiful purple and yellow butterfly fluttered around my head.

"Hey, I was hoping you'd come by the pool," I said.

The butterfly took off and landed near the top of the maple tree in the Hasslers' yard.

I rubbed my hands together. Sticky green mucus began oozing across my palms.

"I'll meet you up there," I called.

Slurp, slurp, slurp. I climbed straight up the trunk of the maple tree. This green stuff works better than suction cups, I thought.

The purple and yellow butterfly flew over and sat on my nose. I grinned at it. "I'm glad we're friends," I said. "I'd hate to spend the *whole* day with Carl."

The butterfly beat its wings together.

"I never could have climbed this high before I met you," I told the butterfly. "You were right, Willow. Some parts of being a bug *can* be awesome."

GOT FEAR?

MAKE SURE TO PICK UP ALL THE SPOOKTACULAR TITLES IN R.L. STINE'S GHOSTS OF FEAR STREET: TWICE TERRIFYING TALES SERIES